Burden of Reckoning

Aaron's Kiss Series Book 4

Kathi S. Barton

This is a work of fiction. Names, characters, places, and incidents are products of the author's imagination or are used factiously and are not to be construed as real. Any resemblance to actual events, locations, organizations, or person, living or dead, is entirely coincidental.

WCP

World Castle Publishing
Pensacola, Florida

Copyright © by Kathi S. Barton 2012
ISBN: 9781937593896
First Edition World Castle Publishing January 1, 2012
http://www.worldcastlepublishing.com

Cover Artist: Karen Fuller
Photo used on cover from Shutterstock
Editor: Brieanna Robertson

CHAPTER ONE

"There's a guy out there to see ya, Sam. He says he's been looking for you." Betty Cramer was in early for her shift, which in her case, was something to remark upon. She delivered her news to the person with their head in the oven.

"I'm kind of busy right now; did he say what he wanted?"

Sam had six more pies to bake, four of them with top crusts that were not cooperating. Finally, after cutting out little apples with left over pie crust dough and painting them to the top with a milk and honey mixture, the pies were ready to pop in the hot oven. There were another eighteen crusts to be filled with custard and two with berries. Now was not the time for socializing.

"Nope, just wanted to talk with Sam Hunter and that'd be you, not me, so I didn't ask. Told him you were busy, but he said he'd wait. Kind of a squirrely acting, if you ask me. Bought the last cheese and cherry Danish, though, oh, and a cup of mocha delight."

"Betty, I told you to save that Danish for me, damn it." Sally Jenkins so didn't need another Danish to eat. She was a good fifty pounds overweight. But then both women were overweight and didn't seem to mind. Sam thought it was great that they didn't let society dictate what size clothing they should be wearing.

Both women had worked full-time for Sam's Baked Goods for four years. The three of them were friends, but yet neither Betty nor Sally knew all that much about Sam. And that's just the way Sam liked it. The two women seemed to like working there and usually hung around until closing time at five to walk home together. Sam owned the shop and the building. It worked out perfectly because she could work anytime she needed to and then go up to bed.

"Tell the mystery man I'll be another ten. And take those cupcakes out to be boxed up please. That lady from Becca's should be here soon to get them. She might need some help taking them out to her car. Hopefully, it's not one of those sub compact thingies."

The cupcakes were why the pies were not done. A place called Becca's Place had called Monday morning, ordering ten dozen of the suckers for a birthday party and, "oh could you please make them half for a girl and the other half for a boy?" the lady had asked. She was nice and even offered to pay more, but still...who needed ten dozen cupcakes for a kid's birthday party? Kids must have a lot of cousins with a big friggin' family, Sam thought with a snort. She couldn't remember the last kid she'd talked too, much less enough of them to need ten dozen cakes.

Sam was another fifteen minutes before she could go out and talk with the man. The shop was really busy at this time of the morning, as always. People stopping by on their way to work had become a habit, and one that paid off really well for Sam's little shop. The coffee was hot and the baked goods fresh and really rich and tasty. And the staff was if nothing else, honest about the food—maybe too honest sometimes.

She noticed that Betty was sharing a cookie with one of the patrons at the counter again.

"Hello there. Sorry about the wait. What can I do for you?" Sam was just throwing the towel she was drying her hands on to the back room when the front door opened and two very beautiful women walked in.

She glanced their way, but didn't really register them physically. Mentally, she felt them. They were different than the others in the room, the humans in the room. But she didn't focus on that, as they seemed to not pose any threat. Yet. But the man waiting to speak to her, he radiated anger, mistrust, and a profound hatred toward women. It was coming off him in waves. Sam took a cautious step toward him to maneuver him closer to the door, and hopefully out.

"I wanted to speak to Sam Hunter. I've waited long enough and I'll not be put off by someone who is certainly not him. Now, this might work on other people, he putting them off and all, but I'm not other people, girly. Not some piece of ass of his that thinks her crap don't stink."

Sam looked around the room to see if they were being heard. The women looked like they might be able to hear, but the others didn't seem to notice. She couldn't touch the man's mind; it was filled with too much red haze caused from anger. She gave the others a small push to leave the store quickly. All of them did, of course, except the women. Sam pushed a little harder.

The man was big and imposing, but that didn't bother Sam. She had been taking care of herself for a while now. Size really didn't matter to her. Not when you came prepared like she did to every situation, especially with the nice equalizer in the waist band of her jeans. Sam was an expert shot and she kept in shape too.

"First of all and most importantly, I am Sam Hunter, and secondly, I am no man's piece of ass. Now, you either state your business with me, or you can turn yourself around and leave. Please don't let the door hit you where the sun doesn't shine. I've got things to do." Sam moved again, this time toward him.

"No, I don't think so. You aren't a man. And if you think that I'm going to take some woman's word about man's business then you'd better think again. Women like you give nice, respectable women a bad name. And as far as I'm concerned, women do not work outside the home —"

"Very good, jackass, you get to go to the head of the gender recognition class. You have a very high opinion of yourself, don't you? Doesn't matter. Now, if you don't mind, as owner of this business, I have work to do." Her voice was low and menacing, not much more than a whisper. But she knew he had heard.

She started to turn away from him. Sometimes, she thought the best way to deal with a bully was to walk away. She got no further than turned around when he spoke again. This time, his voice was loud, carrying to everyone in the room.

"Sam Hunter took my wife, lured her away from her duties to me and my sons. I heard the son of a bitch was a big man, not some sexpot pretending her life has meaning when she ain't got no man to tell her what to do." He grabbed for her arm. "Don't you dare turn your back on me, bitch. Someone should teach you some manners. And by God, I'm just the man to do it."

Sam tensed up and turned around again to look at the man. With a quick glance at Betty, Sam gave her a small nod. For a big woman, Betty could move like the wind when she needed to. She came around the counter and tried to usher the two women out of the line of fire and into the kitchen. They, of course, wouldn't budge. Betty went to the phone and made a quick call to the police. Sam knew this was not going to end pleasantly and she didn't want the law to say she'd done anything wrong.

"Get your filthy hands off me or I'll move them for you. I don't know who you're talking about, but again, I'm Sam Hunter. This is my shop, I bake. I want you to fucking leave, right now. My employee has called the police. And as of right now, I don't know your name. Leaving would do you a world of good."

Sam moved to the left so the man had to turn around and keep his back to the women in the shop. If he got violent, then they would be fairly safe from him. At least she hoped so. She knew they weren't human, as least not full human, but she wasn't sure if they were immortal or not. But Sam knew that Betty and Sally were, and bullets killed mortals.

"Paula Ship, my wife. You're gonna tell me everything I wanna know, bitch. I'm betting you know just where she is. You tell me or else, and I don't care if you are a female. Someone should have taught you manners for a man a long time ago. Right now, you fucking bitch."

Sam suddenly remembered Mrs. Ship. She had been in the shop several weeks ago buying a cake for her son's birthday. She'd been nervous and timid every time someone got close to her. When she moved her arm, Sam had seen the bruises, lots of bruises.

Sam had reached out to the woman mentally and felt her terror of being late and that if she was then she would be beaten for it. Sam also caught glimpses of her being chained to the heater in the kitchen and the length of it being just long enough for her to reach the stove, refrigerator, and the sink. There were other times when one or both of her sons would knock her around. The husband, the man standing before Sam, had taught the sons the way he'd been taught, that women were to be disciplined at all costs.

Sam realized that it would never occur to this man that his wife might have left on her own if she could have. Women like Paula, to his way of thinking, were too stupid to make any decisions of their own. They needed a man, a man like him, to make all the life choices for them. Women like her needed a man to keep them in line and tell them what to do, even if it meant knocking them around a bit now and then just to keep them reminded of who it was in charge. Sam hated this man.

"I don't know where your wife is. And frankly, I don't care either. And as nice as I'm sure her life was living with you, maybe she is better off gone. Like I said, the police have been called and they will be here shortly. Why don't you do us all a favor and leave right now I won't press any charges." She didn't need to press charges. Sam had her own form of punishment in mind.

Sam didn't lie, ever; it was never worth it. There was always the possibility that you'd get caught and she didn't want to have to remember what she said to each person. But she really didn't know where Mrs. Ship was, at least at that very moment she didn't. When Sam had helped Paula to get away, Sam had taken her to an underground system that hid her and others like her away from the abuse. Once they entered that part of their lives, Sam never saw or heard from them again. She knew it was safer for all of them that way.

When Mr. Ship pulled out his gun and pointed it straight at Sam's chest and smiled, she didn't so much as flinch or look at the others in the room. When unfamiliar magic started to flow, Sam threw it back to the sender and felt the immediate withdrawal from one of the women. She didn't know who had tried, but this was her store and her rules.

"Mr. Ship, did you hear me? The police have been called and I'm asking you again to leave here now. I don't know where your wife is. I don't know where you got your information either, but you came here looking for a man and ended up with me. Maybe you should go home and cut your losses. This isn't worth jail time if your wife left you. I don't want to have to hurt you, but I will if you don't listen to me. Now, I'm telling you again to leave."

Sam knew that he was not going to leave. She also knew that he had full intentions of killing her and everyone else in the room until he got the information he wanted. She watched for the slightest movement, the indicator that said when he was about to shoot. When it came, she moved to counterattack, keep everyone safe, and if all possible, keep herself not dead.

When he raised the gun to fire, Sam lunged toward him, knocking his gun away from her chest with a hand to his wrist, knocking it and the gun toward the floor. She knew that she had to disarm him or he would pull the other gun she knew he had hidden in his back. Someone was going to get hurt. She hoped it wasn't anyone she knew. Just as she started to throw him to the left and then to the floor, he pulled the trigger, the sound of it like thunder in the tiny room. The slight pain registered, but she didn't have time right now to deal with it. Sam still needed to get him disarmed and everyone to safety.

Sam brought her foot down hard along his shin, tearing skin and grinding her booted heel across his shin and into the top of his foot. Then she slammed her elbow into his ribs, causing him to drop the gun. When he tried to grab a handful of her hair to jerk her around, she brought her forehead back then forward to hit his jaw, breaking the mandible and knocking him unconscious. He dropped like a dead weight. Sam staggered a little from the impact of hitting his head with hers and then sat down hard on the floor. She needed to lean back against the wall to take an inventory of her own body.

The two women rushed her and she raised her hand to stop them. She was in no mood to meet and greet right now. They stopped dead in their tracks. Sam grinned. Okay, she thought, probably should have dropped the gun and wiped off the blood first. If someone had pointed a bloodied, armed hand at her, she probably would have stopped too. Looking down at her leg, she realized she had been shot.

"Well shit a brick and build a house." The women moved closer. "Don't touch me. I ...just don't touch me. Oh God, I'm gonna be sick."

Sam backed closer to the wall again and crawled her way up, using it to pull herself to a standing position. Then she staggered her way to the back room, her hand covering her mouth as she went.

Blood was soaking her jeans now. Also, it was all the way down her leg and into her boot. There was a thin trail of it following her as she walked away. The wall she had leaned against had a bloody handprint, as did the counter and the doorway to the back where she had had to stop and steady herself. She knew that people wouldn't notice, but right now, her late breakfast was coming back for a second appearance. When she had sicked up everything in the tiny bathroom off the kitchen, she made her way upstairs to her apartment.

Lt. David Wolff showed up about five minutes later. Sam could see his cruiser as it pulled into the lot from her bedroom window. The light flashing probably told the entire neighborhood. She went down the stairs and watched from her vantage point just inside the foyer—the area between her apartment and the kitchen.

The man, Mr. Ship, had been tied to a chair in her kitchen with duct tape, and Betty was standing over him with a large cast iron skillet in her hand, arms crossed over her ample chest. Sam wondered where the pan had come from, but realized that was the least of her problems. He was still unconscious, or at least he was now. Sam smiled again. Betty could be a bit overprotective of Sam when it wasn't really necessary. But Sam loved her for it.

"Where's Sam at, Betty? Is she all right?" David demanded again. "You didn't do a very good job of cleaning up the blood; there are streaks of it everywhere. And since Mr. Ship here has his head bashed in and would be dead with that amount of blood loss, I'm assuming it must be Sam who's bleeding."

Sam had known David for nearly three years now. She was pretty sure he knew what she did on the side, rescuing women and children from an abusive situation and making sure they were safe. But they stayed out of each other's way. This was the first time someone had come to her about their missing family and she didn't like knowing someone knew where she worked and lived. She would have to be more careful in the future and also see how Mr. Ship found her so quickly. If he could, then she was reasonably sure others could as well. Sam was sure other spouses would be just as curious as Mr. Ship had been.

"Don't rightly know what you're talking about, Officer Wolff. Sam ain't been here all day." He just looked at her, and then at the man in the chair. Sam had to stifle a laugh. Betty, it seemed, could be just as stubborn as her boss when it suited her.

13

"You telling me you did this? You knocked this man unconscious and tied him to the chair? What did he do, Betty? Make fun of the cookies you sell? Not bloody likely. Please tell me where Sam is. You don't want me calling in other officers to search this place, do you?"

"I'm here, I did it." Sam walked into her kitchen. "Sally, can you see that these two women are taken care of for me, please?" When no one moved, not even her employees, she huffed before she turned back to David. "He was here for some woman named Paula, his wife, he said. He drew a gun and I disarmed him. And just in the event that he tried anything while I was gone, Betty here...subdued him."

Sam noticed that David looked at the two women and realized he knew them, knew them quite well, it seemed. Sam closed her eyes against the drain the pain was causing her. It didn't help that she had to keep blocking one or both of the women from tapping into her head.

"We were here, David. We saw the whole thing, so I'm sure you'd like us to stick around a bit longer, right?" the dark-haired woman informed David. "It was self-defense, she wasn't lying about that. He drew on her first. She's also shot, bleeding pretty good too." Sam glared at the woman, hoping she would shut the hell up.

Sam had changed her pants and although she was limping, there was no telltale sign that she had been wounded. At least she hoped so. She had wrapped the wound up before pulling on a fresh pair of pants. The wound was deep and the bullet was still in it, but she didn't have time to mess with it right now. As soon as everyone left, she would fix it. She just hoped the blood didn't seep through before the cop noticed and the nosey women left. Sam thought that it was a lost cause as soon as David spoke again.

"Shot? What happened here, Sam? Where are you hurt? Where did he shoot you? Damn it, woman, why the hell didn't you tell me first thing?" Sam saw David's nose flare and she realized that he couldn't smell her. Good, at least something was going right.

Sam knew that David was a were and could probably smell blood as soon as he walked in the tiny shop. Sam had hoped that he would have thought it was Mr. Ship's and not hers. No hope for that, thanks to little Miss Helpful Customer. Sam turned back to her to glare once again. She wasn't ever going to get a discount, she thought.

"Nope, I'm fine. This nice lady is mistaken, nothing wrong with me." Sam wished that everyone would go away so she could go back upstairs. "If you've come here to pick up the cupcakes, then Sally can help you with that, and out of the front door."

She was being rude, but at this point, really didn't care. Pain was pulsing through her at an alarming rate. And she was afraid she was going to be sick again.

The bossy woman was not the least bit intimidated by Sam's rudeness, nor by her look, it appeared to Sam. The woman simply stepped forward, making Sam make a hasty retreat back a few steps. When she reached out and grabbed where the bullet had entered Sam's thigh, jamming her thumb into the wound itself, pain shot through Sam like a knife, and she moaned from the fresh pain, blood oozing from the now opened wound.

"You fucking bitch," Sam hissed at her. Dizziness swamped her and she reached out and grabbed the first thing she could reach, which happened to be the woman who had hurt her. Now Sam was swamped with pain and the woman's thoughts. They were both dizzying and profoundly scary, this woman's thoughts. Sam let her go and slumped to the floor.

"Yes, would you like to tell me again how I was wrong about you being wounded? You've lost a good deal of blood and you need medical attention before you pass out. Now, do I take you to the hospital or do we call an ambulance? Because, either way, you are getting that looked at even if I have to take your ass there myself."

The woman hadn't raised her voice, which under normal circumstances would have impressed Sam, but pain was making her short tempered and lightheaded. The images she was pulling from the woman showed her to be a mate to a vampire. She had two children and she was one powerful bitch, along with way too much information for her to sort right now.

"I want you to mind your own damned business is what's going to happen. I'm fine," Sam said with a hiss of pain. When Sam turned back to David, she said, "Mr. Ship came into my shop demanding to talk to Sam Hunter, a male Sam Hunter, and I told him I didn't know who he was talking about. He pulled a gun, it went off, and I disarmed him, end of story. Now, I am closed. It's been an eventful morning, and I'm going home." She turned to leave, but got no more than two feet way when she slipped into a black void, knowing, just knowing that that nosey woman had something to do with it.

CHAPTER TWO

When Sam woke up, she looked around the room trying to figure out where she was, but as nothing looked familiar, she knew that she was not home. The room was huge and beautifully decorated; everything was old but very well maintained. The only thing she was actually concerned with was her lack of gun and that her body hurt beyond all good reason. The rest, she decided she could fix.

There was an IV in her left arm that was hooked up to a glucose bag. She was also dressed in a nightshirt that she had never seen before and was not even going to think about who might have dressed her in it. There was a phone by the bed, but until she knew where she was, using it was out of the question. No telling who or what might be at the other end.

Sam carefully pulled the needle from the back of her hand. Then she began a survey of the damage to herself before swinging her legs to the side of the bed. She fought through the dizziness by taking deep breaths while her eyes were closed. The pain she could almost manage, but it was hard—the pain in her leg was incredible. The bullet must have hit one of the deep muscles in her thigh. But running her hand lightly over the bandage, she realized that someone had removed the bullet and had stitched her up. She knew from the touch that the last person to touch the bandage was a male, a vampire. She worked slowly to get her butt to the edge of the mattress so that standing up would be easier, at least in theory, she thought with a wary grin.

When she was finally able to stand with the aid of one of the posts on the big bed, she had to really concentrate on not passing out. Using the walls as support, she made her way slowly to what she hoped was the bathroom; it was the closest doorway from the bed. If it was not then she was going to have a hard time explaining to whoever owned this house why she was in the closet. When she opened the door, she nearly whimpered when she discovered she was right, and went inside.

As she eased herself down onto the toilet seat to rest, she laid her head on the double vanity to wait for the room to stop spinning and hopefully the pain to recede at least a little. She really didn't hold out much hope of either happening anytime soon—she hadn't even had the energy to lift the lid, much less get up and move again to pee. As she lay there contemplating on how she was going to get home when she couldn't even pee, she heard someone clear their throat close to where the door was. She didn't move to speak, but stayed where she was.

"I'd like my clothes, if you don't mind. And I noticed my gear is missing. So if you'd be so kind as to give it back, I'd appreciate that. I'm sorry about the mess here, but as I don't know you or where I'm at, I'll assume this is one of the two women's houses from...is today still Thursday? Anyway, I didn't ask to be brought here, so I can't be held responsible for what happens while I am here." Sam knew she was babbling. It was either that or scream down the house.

When nothing was forthcoming, she turned her head slightly without lifting it to the figure in the door jam.

He was a smallish man, not tiny, just small of stature, and he was holding a very large bed tray filled with what smelled like coffee. Her belly gave a slight jump at the thought of food. Shit! He continued to stare at her as if he couldn't believe she was in his bathroom. Quirking a brow at him, she wondered if he was human.

"Well? Do I have a wart on my head or do you not speak English? Sprechen Sie Deutsch? How about Parlez-vous du français? ¿Habla usted español?, Вы говорите на русском языке? You need to work with me here, buddy. I hurt like hell and I'd like to go home."

"English. I speak English. The others as well, but I prefer English. Miss, are you well? Should you be up as yet? The doctor said it would be several days yet before you would be up and about. Not to mention that you wouldn't even be awake until at least tomorrow. I have found that Doctor Reilly is rarely incorrect in these matters. Shall I call him back and inform him of your recovery?"

Wow, Sam thought, he sounded just like her tenth grade English teacher, all prim and proper. "No, no need to call him or anyone else for that matter. But you should know that...well, I'm really a stubborn sort. And I seldom follow orders. They make me crazy. I'd really like my gun and my clothes back." Sam was not going to tell this man that she had been hurt worse and this was not her first gunshot wound, nor would it likely be her last. She just stared at him until he answered.

"I do not believe them to be dry as yet, miss. There was quite a bit of blood on them so I washed them twice in hopes of getting them clean for you. There was nothing I could do for your boots, however. I believe them to be completely ruined. Doctor Mercer, a human doctor, was quite adamant about you having plenty to drink when you awoke. I have brought you some juice and things for you to drink to replenish your blood supply. I think…I believe that you have opened the wound again. He will be most displeased about that. Her ladyship as well, I'm sure."

As he fussed about the bedroom after laying down the tray, he continued his one-sided conversation with her. Sam tuned him out and tried to figure out the complexities of getting up, peeing, and going back into the room and getting dressed to leave. She felt it was just too much right now and stayed where she was, at least for a few more minutes.

"Miss? Miss, are you all right? You have been laying there for the past twenty minutes and I am beginning to get very concerned after your welfare. Would you like some help? I'm quite capable of rendering you aid if you so desire."

"Clothes! I want my friggin' clothes." She shouted at him, her pain making her short tempered. As an afterthought she said, "I'm sorry. It's not your fault that I'm a bitch when I'm in pain. Well, I'm always a bitch, but that's still no reason to shout at you. Could you please give me my clothes and my gear?"

"Yes, I'll retrieve them post haste. Just let me help…no, I can see that you would rather do it yourself. Yes, well if you insist, I will go downstairs — to the laundry room."

~~~

Duncan had been startled by her glare. He didn't frighten easily, especially in this household, but the young miss frankly scared him a little. Her ladyship was going to be very upset at the turn of events. He almost hoped that she wouldn't be in the kitchen when he went in to get the young woman's clothes.

Duncan had heard the little alarm that sounded in the kitchen when Sam crossed the threshold into the bath. He had been surprised by the sound, not because he had forgotten about it, but Doctor Mercer had assured him it would be several days, maybe even a week before the wounded woman would be concisions, much less up and about, yet here she was. It had only been a mere six hours since she had been brought in by the policeman and her ladyship, and now the wounded girl was moving around. He was worried about her pallor and the fresh blood seeping from the wound.

Doc Mercer was a human doctor, that was to say he was human and a doctor for humans. Duncan himself had called to see to the young woman and her wounds. The doctor had wanted to take her to the hospital, but her ladyship wouldn't budge on this. Doctor Mercer had asked that Sam be put into a slight comalike state to help her heal and to keep her from doing what she was doing right now, leaving the estate. Lady Sara had agreed and had simply touched the woman and rendered her into a deep sleep. *No, the lady of the house was not going to be happy*, Duncan thought.

Sara was sitting in the kitchen enjoying her cup of tea. When Duncan saw her, he nearly turned around and left the room again, but she looked up just then and saw him.

"Duncan, Penny said that you took a tray up to the young woman. She can't possibly be awake already. What's going on?" Duncan didn't like the tone she had, but knew there was no hope for either him or the girl upstairs.

"She isn't only awake, my lady, but she has gotten to the bathroom without assistance. And although her wound had opened again, she is now requesting, and quite strongly I should add, that I bring the young miss her clothing. She wishes to leave as soon as she is dressed, I believe. Shall I drive her home?"

"Leave? Well, we'll just see about that. And no, you most certainly are not driving her home. She is going to recuperate here if I have to shoot her in the other leg for her to do it."

Duncan thought this was highly unlikely as Lady Sara didn't even own a gun, but thought it wise to keep his mouth closed.

Sara took the now neatly folded clothes from Duncan and threw them back into the laundry room. She was heading up the grand staircase before he realized he hadn't had the chance to ask Sara about the "gear" the girl had mentioned. When Lady Sara was like this, he found it best to move out of her way.

Oh my, Duncan thought, *this can't bode well for*...Well, he was not sure who would win this battle. He decided to call this round two, as her ladyship had won the first by putting the woman, Sam, into a deep sleep and had her brought here. Who knew how this was going to turn out? He thought things had been lively before, but he believed this woman might be able to hold her own against her ladyship. Chuckling to himself, Duncan picked up the clothing and began to fold it neatly again. Yes, he thought, things were about to be stirred up once again.

CHAPTER THREE

Luckily for Sam, she had turned her head to look before she spoke this time. She was ready and willing to blast the next person who came through the door if they didn't have her stuff. She was still sitting on the toilet and neither her temperament nor the level of pain had improved much. Truth be told, she was hurting badly enough that she was actually considering getting back into the big bed and dying.

There were two kids standing in the door to the bathroom staring at her. The three of them observed one another for a good minute before the boy spoke. The girl was quiet, but she was not without activity. Sam felt her poke at her mind harder. The boy had tried, but had given up as soon as he hit her barrier. This was by and far the strangest household she'd ever been in.

"You know, you're dripping blood on the floor. I don't think that's too healthy. My daddy said that blood is an important part of living for us."

Ignoring the blood comment, Sam glared as she spoke. "Is this place like Grand Central Station or something? Yes, I'm very aware that I'm bleeding on the floor, but if someone hadn't have brought me here in the first place then I would be dripping on my own floor, not yours. Where's that guy, the one with the tray? He was supposed to bring me my sh...my stuff."

She'd had more visitors in this one room than she'd had at her apartment in two years. Actually, when she thought about that, it was sort of sad. She wasn't going there right now; she had to get out of here. The girl poked harder at Sam's wall. She thought about hitting her back, but with the pain, was afraid she'd hurt the girl.

"No. It's just a house. You mean Mr. Duncan? I guess he's in the kitchen. He's always in the kitchen. He keeps the house for us, him and Miss Penny."

The boy seemed so serious and Sam wondered what he was. The other one, his sister, she assumed, because looking at the two of them together left no doubt in anyone's mind that they were blood related, looked as if she was straining at something really hard. Sam knew she couldn't break through. Sam had a great deal more practice and she might have been a little more powerful in that department.

"You all right, kid? You look like you're about to explode or poop your pants. And as this one pointed out, I doubt either of those is too healthy. Neither is either of them going to make the owner very happy."

"I can't read you. Why is that?" the little girl asked. Sam had no doubt the kid was used to popping in and out of minds like a game, but not her.

"First of all, I'm not a book, so you not being able to 'read' me is a given. Secondly, has anyone ever told you it's very rude to try and cop a feel into someone's psyche without permission or provocation? I haven't given you either, so mind your own business, kid. Thirdly, and I only bring this up because you are still trying, someone stronger than you could hurt you if you aren't a little more careful with your searching. You aren't gentle. People shouldn't be able to feel you enter and search. What you're doing is what I think of as mind rape, so back off, kid."

"You aren't supposed to be able to feel me. Why can you feel me and nobody else has been able to before?" she groused as she stopped her foot.

Sam merely raised her brow. "Go ask your mother. I'm sure she has an answer for you. At least she seems to think she does about everything else anyway. Don't you?"

Sam looked up at the door across the room to stare at who she assumed was the children's mother. They looked too much like her not to be. Sam had known she was there, just as Sam had known the little girl was in her mind. There was something "otherworldly" about the boy, more so than the two women from today and the little girl standing there so defiantly.

Sam did have a tight hold on her mind, extremely tight. She had taught herself how to block people's touches just after her mom had been killed when she was younger. Some people just touched what she left out for them to find, a sort of open book of useless information and tidbits that anyone could find out about her without much effort. Then there were the people who bumped the wall and tried as hard as they could to breach it. The harder they tried, the more painful it became for them. Eventually, they would have to stop their efforts. Others, like the little girl, kept trying until they either exhausted themselves, or got a nose bleed, sometimes worse. Sam thought the little girl must be fairly strong, as she didn't seem to be bothered by either just yet.

"I see you've met my children. This is Lizzy and Mac. Say hello to Sam Hunter, children, then go to the kitchen. I'd like to have a few words with Miss Hunter in private for a moment."

"Oh no, that means you are in for some serious yelling. That's what my dad says when she uses that tone with him." Mac made his what turned out to be a very accurate prediction and sped from the room, chasing his sister and laughing at the top of his lungs.

"Cute kid. Must take after his dad." Sam was hurting. But she had to get out of this place. And she didn't care much for the bossy woman in from of her. Sitting up with as much dignity as she could muster while sitting on a toilet and bleeding, she looked Sara straight in the eye.

"You aren't very grateful, are you? Doesn't matter, I want you to get back into the bedroom and get off of that leg. You have lost more blood and it is doubtful you could stand to lose much more." The lady of the house stood over her with her hands on her hips. Her tone said, "I'm lord of this house and all obey." Well, not Sam. As she had told Duncan, she didn't do well with orders.

"I'd like my clothes and my gear. I have asked for it several times now, and I'm frankly sick of doing so. I didn't ask to come here. I don't want to be here, and I'd like you to back the fuck off. Speaking of that, why the hell am I here?"

It wasn't as if Sam was used to getting her own way, but she did know her own strengths. She could also tell that this woman didn't usually strong arm people, but was normally very nice. She just didn't like to be told no and she was worried about Sam. She couldn't help it, Sam snorted. It was time to take action.

"I am the lady of this house and you would do well to…" The woman suddenly stopped and crumbled to a heap on the floor.

Turnabout was fair play, Sam thought with a grin. "Yeah. Not so much fun getting knocked out when you want to make a grand exit, is it?" Sam knew she couldn't hear her, but she felt good for saying it all the same.

Sam stood and white-fisted the vanity before taking a slow step into the bedroom. The wound had stopped bleeding while she had been sitting still and not moving. Now that she was up, it was open and bleeding again. Nausea had her belly tighten up, but she knew there was nothing left in it to sick up. Sam stepped over the crumpled woman and left her lying there.

It took her a good two minutes to make it to the top of the staircase when she needed to rest again. She was afraid to sit down, fearing that she wouldn't be able to get up again if she did. Sam was losing blood quickly now, and weakness and dizziness had become her new best friend. She decided to find a phone before tackling the stairs that would surely lead to freedom. She looked around, thinking in a house this big, there had to be phone on this level.

On the fourth try—how many friggin' bedrooms does this place have anyway?—she found a study of sorts. There was a desk, or at least she figured it was a desk, under that mound of papers and files, and a nice chair sitting several inches away from its messy counterpart as if were afraid. Sam certainly was. She sat in the overstuffed chair to use the phone to call for someone to come and get her. But first things first, she needed an address. She started looking over the mess of papers on the desk to find one.

~~~

Aaron MacManus had been trying to contact Sara for the past twenty minutes and was not having any luck. He began his ascend to the upper floors from his lair when he smelled the blood. He began his search in earnest for her now. He knew the blood was not Sara or the children's, but he worried all the same. When he walked into his office some ten minutes later, he saw a young woman was asleep in his chair, or at least he assumed she was asleep. He knew whatever had happened while he'd been at rest, this woman was hurt badly.

Aaron didn't know what had happened today, so he didn't know who she was, why she was here, or more importantly, where his mate Sara was. He started to move forward when he noticed that Mac was sitting in the chair across from the desk watching the woman intently.

"Mac, son, do you know where your mom is?" He spoke softly, not wanting to alarm anyone, especially his son. Aaron whispered because he knew that his son would still be able to hear him.

"She was on the floor in the bathroom in the red room. Duncan put her in the pink room on the bed, I think. I'm pretty sure this lady did something to her. She's okay, Mom, I mean, but I don't know about this one. I think she is very weak, and she is leaving blood everywhere she goes like she's got lots to spare or something. I told her what you said about blood being important and all, but she didn't pay any attention. I've been keeping an eye on her until the doctor comes again. Duncan is calling him now."

"Good job, son, thank you. Who is she and do you know why she's bleeding?" Aaron wanted to go to Sara, but he didn't feel comfortable leaving his son with a stranger, unconscious or not. He was aware that if Duncan felt his mate was all right to leave on the bed, then she would be fine. But if this woman had hurt his mate — well, hell would be paid.

"Don't know. She's pretty, huh?"

Aaron walked toward his desk to check the pulse of the girl. It was weak, but not dangerously so, not at the moment at any rate. He could tell, though, that if she lost much more blood, she would be dead soon. She really was pretty, beautiful really.

Her hair was blondish brown and pulled back into a messy half braid. What he could see of it pulling loose; it looked to be pin straight and very long. Her skin was pale, almost white against the chair's dark color. Her lips looked drained as well, more than likely due to the amount of blood she had lost than her lack of normal good health. She was slumped in the chair at an odd angle and her leg, the one that was, or had been, bleeding was ramrod straight out from her body. He looked at what she had in her hands and noticed that she had picked up some of his papers.

When he glanced at the desk, he noticed that she had taken it upon herself to organize some of the piles he had haphazardly thrown all over it. The piles she had started were in date order and in neat stacks. They were also in alphabetical order by company. He was not sure how long she had been in there before succumbing to the blood loss, but she had gotten more done in that time than he had been able to accomplish is the five years he had been Master of the Realm. He just couldn't seem to get a handle on the amount of mess that had been left to him when he had taken over from the previous master.

He looked back at the girl and was surprised to see her eyes open. They were the most startling shade of purple Aaron had ever seen, like a rich amethyst with the sun streaming through it.

"I...I would like to go home. I need an address to have...to have someone come and get me. Can you tell me where I am? And I...my gear, where is my gear?" Aaron looked at his son to see if he knew what she was referring to. When Mac shrugged, Aaron turned back to the girl. "I want to go home. I...I don't feel so good. You're very nice-looking, did you know that?"

"I don't think you're in any shape to leave just yet, young lady. Your pulse is very weak and you've lost a great deal of blood. I'm going to pick you up and take you back to your room, and then I understand the doctor is coming to check on you." Aaron spoke to her slowly and calmly, even though his heart was pounding in his chest.

He had opened himself to her and found her to be in incredible pain, and much weaker than he had first thought.

"Don't touch me! I don't like to be touched. I don't want to stay. I want my gear now."

Aaron could feel the her energy draining from her and her burst of anger just then had taken a great deal more out of her than she had to spare. "Mac, I want you to go and get whatever she came here with, and bring it to me now, please?" Aaron didn't take his eyes off of the girl, but calming her down was imperative. Her heart rate was slowing to a dangerously low rate now and he was not at all sure the doctor was going to make it. "And tell Duncan to call Thomas and get him here ASAP, all right, son?"

Mac was off like a rocket. Aaron knew that Mac would do just as he had asked. Aaron also knew that like him, Mac would be able to hear her heart rate slowing and her body weakening.

"Miss, I need to get you to a bed. You're going to die if we don't get you medical attention immediately, do you understand?" Even as he was talking to her, he was leaning in to pick her up, sliding his arms beneath her legs. He felt her try to struggle to get away and he wondered at a fear so great that even this close to death one would try to get away from a simple touch. The effort cost her a great deal, opening the wound that he could tell had started to heal. He could smell the spurt of fresh blood and felt its warmth spreading onto his shirt. Before he had even had a chance to lift her completely, she was nearly unconscious again. But what she had said before slipping away would haunt him for months.

"If your wife would have left me alone, I'd already be dead, you know? I want to be dead. I'm so very tired. Just let me go...you have no right to...I'm not any of your concern. There isn't...anyone left to care for me."

CHAPTER FOUR

Tucker James was not a happy man, or in this circumstance, a happy vampire. He had been trying to get to see the master of this realm for nearly two weeks now and today, when he had an appointment, he was being stood up. Tuck, as some called him, was hungry too.

It seemed that there had been some sort of a medical emergency and he had been put into the little room and forgotten about. He stood up to leave. It had been nearly three hours since his arrival and he needed to either make contact, or leave the area. It was the law of this realm to report to the master immediately if one wanted to move into his realm. That was fine and dandy if a person could let him know somehow before he discovered it on his own and killed you, Tuck thought with a frown. Of course, he had heard that Master MacManus was a fair man and that was, more than anything, what Tucker wanted.

Tucker walked into the main hallway to look around. He had been led down this hall when he came in and wanted to see if he could find the man who had let him in—Duncan, he had called himself. But there was no one in sight, so he began walking and followed the noises of the house when he happened upon two kids who looked to be about five or so.

"Excuse me, but can you tell me where I might find an adult, a Mr. MacManus or Mr. Duncan, please? I had an appointment with the master, but I think I might have gotten the wrong day or something. I know that there are things going on, but I'd like to see if I can come back sometime soon."

"They're upstairs right now. Come with me and I'll take you up. Daddy is with her and so is the doctor. Mr. Duncan is beside himself with worry. Daddy said that, not me. I don't even know what it means. Sam is hurt and the doctor is here." The little girl jumped up to take him upstairs.

As soon as she touched his hand, Tucker realized his mistake. She could feel him and everything about him. He pulled his hand free and winked at her. Powers like hers could cause all sorts of problems if the little girl didn't learn to control them. He felt her touch his mind and he pushed back.

"Thanks, kid, but I think we'd both be better off if you didn't touch me with your powers just now. I like my secrets just where they are."

She led him up to a bedroom where the door was wide open and everyone was standing around the in the center of the room. Tucker couldn't see this Sam person, but figured he must be pretty important to the family to have this many people working to save him. He thought it would be great to have someone care enough to go to this much trouble for. Just as suddenly as the thought popped into his mind, he pushed it away. He had no time for self-pity, not if he was planning to make a fresh start.

"If she won't take the blood, she will die. I don't know how many more times I can say that to you. No blood equals death. She's lost a great deal, Aaron, a great deal. And she's not human. At least I don't think she is, but who knows anymore. Since coming to this realm, I'm not even sure what I am anymore."

Thomas Reilly, Duncan had told Tucker, a vampire and a doctor, had been there for as long as Tucker had, trying to save the girl's life, it appeared. It looked to him like they were trying to get her to sip from one of them. Vampire blood was very strong and would heal even a human if they could get it into them. And this being was proving to be quite stubborn if the faces were any indication, not to mention the tone of the voices.

"Damn it, try harder, Thomas. She will not die; I owe her for that nice nap she put me in today," a very beautiful woman said, worry coloring her voice.

"Dad, this man wants to see you. He's been here forever and ever." The little girl tugged on Tucker's arm and practically threw him into the din. He'd completely forgotten about her. A man, the girl's father, Tucker presumed, stood suddenly from the end of the bed, turned toward his daughter, and frowned. Power and something surged from the man, a power so strong Tuck staggered slightly from it.

"I'm sorry, I completely forgot. As you can see, we have a bit of a problem here. She has been shot and my wife brought her here to heal. But it seems she is just too stubborn to stay put. She's lost a great deal of blood and now she isn't cooperating with the doctor." He might as well have been talking to the floor for all Tucker paid him any heed.

Aaron was looking to the girl as he spoke, so Tucker's eyes drifted to the figure on the bed. The "*he*" he'd been so sure of downstairs was a very beautiful, very weak *she*. He took a step toward her, then another before he realized he had walked by the master's hand that he had extended to him.

"I'm sorry, I...he isn't a man. She's...I..." Tucker looked at the master.

Something was wrong. Not just with the girl, the woman really, but with the scents in the room, her scent, as a matter of fact. Tuck didn't know why, but he suddenly needed to touch her. And her scent was so strong that it surprised him. He was amazed at how strong the urge was to throw everyone out of the room and care for her himself. He also wanted her. Wanted to mark her and take her as his. That was a terrifying as it was intriguing.

"You're Tucker James, aren't you? I'm Aaron MacManus, Master of this Realm. You want to be a part of my realm, if I remember correctly." Tucker nodded. "This young woman is dying and I'd like to save her life, but she's being incredibly stubborn. Why don't you try, Tucker? She needs to have our blood, but she won't take it, at least from none of us, and we've all tried. If we don't do something soon, she'll be dead by morning."

Tucker only heard about half of what Aaron had said to him. The only thing that registered was that she was dying and needed to sip from someone. He knew instinctively that she couldn't die. That without her, he would die as well.

"No, no she can't...I...no, she cannot die, sire. I'll...I would very much like to try and save her. Save her for you. No, she cannot die."

Tucker moved to the bed and sat down very close to her head. He traced a finger down her cheek and felt that her skin was cold and dry. Tucker reached under her and gently pulled her limp body into his arms, cradling her in his big body and into his warmth; she gave a small, pitiful moan and quieted once more. With a hand under her neck, he tilted her head back as gently as he could. When he had her in a good position, he put his wrist to his mouth and opened his vein with an incisor. Blood welled on his skin, hot and fresh. He put the open wound to her mouth and forced his whole wrist between her pale lips. Leaning in closer, he whispered into her ear, softly begging her to drink from him, to please sip his essence from him. She didn't move for a very long time, didn't drink his life giving blood, and barely breathed. Tucker thought he had failed her as well, when suddenly, she swallowed what was in her mouth, then again when his blood filled her mouth again. It wasn't long before she reached up and held his arm closer to her mouth, but she didn't open her eyes. Relief so profound surged through his body and heart.

"Thank you, Tucker," the master said softly. "When you finish here with Sam, could you please meet me in the downstairs living room? It will be at the bottom of the stairs and to the right; we'll be waiting for you. I can't thank you enough for this, for helping her. I appreciate it. My family appreciates it as well."

He only nodded at him, but didn't take his eyes off the woman in his arms. Aaron had called her Sam. And though it was a strange name for a woman, Tucker thought that it probably suited her better than most girly names would. She looked to be hard and tough, soft and sexy. Sexy was an understatement, he thought, but let it go.

Tucker fed her for another few minutes before he pulled his wrist away and sealed the wound with his own saliva. He then picked her up and tucked her into the bed, bringing the thick covers up and over her warming body. He wanted to join her in the bed and to hold her until she was better, but knew that he couldn't. She didn't know him any more than he knew her. And being a woman, waking up next to a strange man would be scary. But Tuck did know this, Sam was his mate. Someone he had given up on, and now that he had found her, it was too late.

~~~

Aaron stood at the fireplace waiting for the people in his family, his Kiss, to settle. He knew they had questions, and right now he was not sure how to answer them. Tucker had sensed Sam; Aaron knew it as sure as he was standing there. But he also felt his sorrow at doing so. He couldn't wait to talk to the vampire. He wished he had taken the time to read over the brief letter that Tucker had sent to him a few days ago.

"Want to explain to me why we just left a perfect stranger in our upstairs bedroom with a woman who was in our care? I wasn't even aware you had someone coming in tonight, yet you let him heal her. Aaron, what are you not telling me?"

Sara was relieved that Sam was going to live; Aaron could tell that. His mate wanted Sam to heal so that Sara could kick her ass, but to leave her in the care of a vamp they didn't know concerned her. He took her into his arms and held her as he spoke.

"She's his mate. Tucker James came here to ask to be in our realm, and found Sam. That's why she would only take from him and none of the rest of us." Aaron looked to the door just before Tucker walked in.

"She drank, sire. And I have deepened her sleep. I believe she will be fine now. I…I'll be going now. I've changed my mind. If it would please you, I'd like to stay in your realm for a mere fortnight then move on. I won't feed from the humans unless they're willing, nor will I cause you any problems." Tucker hadn't looked at Aaron once. But had delivered his speech looking at the floor in a very subservient way. For some reason, this bothered Aaron more than he could say.

"Come in and sit down, Tucker. I think we should talk about what happened between you and Sam, who I assume you *know* is your mate. You can't leave her now. You've given her your blood. To leave her now would cause you both undue harm and you know that."

Aaron had always liked the straightforward approach. He saw no reason to change his ways now just because this man cringed at his tone. But it did give him pause, the way this man acted, the way he had behaved.

Tucker glanced toward the stairs and then up at the master before dropping his head again. Aaron reached out to touch Tucker's mind and couldn't believe the incredible amount of sorrow there. Pain as well. He could also tell that Tucker was aware of what would happen if he left Sam, but Aaron felt that rather than run from Sam, he was actually trying to protect her from something, or someone. He felt the moment Tucker shut the door on that memory, slammed it shut hard enough that Aaron felt it. Surprised, too, if he was honest. The lock was tight as well as strong.

"No, sire, I mean you no disrespect, but I'm going to leave your home now. Thank you for your time. Missus." At his nod to Sara, he dematerialized from the house.

~~~

Sam woke in the middle of the next day to a black as pitch room as the heavy shades on the house were down against the sunlight. It was hard to tell, but her watch set in military time told her it was fourteen-hundred zero seventeen hours. Her body ached, but was otherwise in better shape than she thought it should be. She tentatively moved her wounded leg and found it to be nearly healed, and she thought fleetingly of who or what might have healed her. The rest of her body seemed to be in fairly good shape as well.

Sam rose to go to the bathroom again, this time without any problems, and peed, and did some light maintenance on her hair and face. Taking the tube of toothpaste on the counter, she squeezed some out on her finger and brushed her teeth that way. She noticed that she had a funny metallic taste in her mouth that was not all that unpleasant, a spicy, hot taste that she wished she could remember. Sam had been around "other" people enough to know that some of them could heal, while others still would destroy. She didn't ponder the *how* of someone healing her. She just wasn't very happy with the end results. Sam did feel that people should really learn to mind their own business. She only hoped that she would have the chance to tell that interfering woman a few more things before she left.

On the back of the toilet, she found her clothes neatly folded and a couple of clean towels. As much as she wanted to get out of there, a nice hot shower sounded too tempting to forgo. Sliding out of the t-shirt she had never seen before and her panties, she turned the taps to full blast and hot enough to pink up her skin. An enjoyable twenty minutes later, she was walking into the kitchen of the mansion.

Duncan let out a small noise and dropped the tea cup and saucer he had just taken out of the dishwasher. It shattered unnoticed on the tile floor when Sam walked into the large, bright kitchen. The older woman, a human, turned quickly to the door to see what had caused him to squeak and drop the china. Her mouth nearly dropped to her ample bosom. Sam grinned. There was no way she was going to try and figure out what they were staring at.

"I'm pretty sure the household knows I'm here. I'm not planning to rob anyone."

Sam had an idea of what she looked like standing there. She'd had a look at herself in the mirror—healthy now and glowing with it. Sam wasn't unaware of her good looks or beauty. Her hair hung loose and damply down and about her shoulders, darkened by the water. When dry, it was a rich golden color. Sam's face was pretty enough, she supposed. Her eyebrows arched over sparkling purple eyes, lashes as long as a man's finger was wide, cheek bones that were high and pink with health. Her nose was small and turned up at the end with a tiny aristocratic tilt. Hundreds of freckles danced across her nose and her cheeks of which she hated. Her lips were full and wide, a natural pink. Her shoulders were broad, and her ample, full breasts balanced her out. Nothing could be seen of her waist or hips as the clothes she had on were way too large and bulky.

"I need an address to call a cab, please? And for the hundredth time, I'd like my gear." They were making her very nervous the way they were staring at her, and she wished that she had a coat and hat to pull on.

"Your gear, miss? All you had with you are the things that you have on now. I'm not sure what else there should have been." Penny had answered as Duncan was still staring at her with his mouth hanging open.

"She means her gun and bullets, Penny." Sam turned at the voice behind her. "David has them. He didn't want to leave them with you in my house with children about. He said that he'd return them to you when you called. He also said you'd have to produce a permit before you got them back."

Ah, Sam thought, *the woman of the house.* Of course. She'd wondered how long it would be before she showed up and started throwing her weight around. Sam turned around and looked at the woman fully.

"Smart man, he's probably thinking someone would shoot you with it. I still need an address so that a cab knows where to come and rescue me. Unless of course you'd like to try and hurt me again first. I'm sure I can be your equal this time. I'm not weak from blood loss."

Duncan hissed at Sam, but she didn't turn to look at him. She was too busy staring daggers at the mistress of the house. Though she had to admit, the woman was giving as good as she got.

"I don't like you very much."

If the woman thought to make Sam back down, or apologize, then she didn't know Sam all that well. She laughed instead. "Well, that's good. I'd hate to think all this animosity and ill will toward you was one-sided." Sam was not much of a socializer, but knew that she was being very nasty to Sara. She didn't know what it was about this beautiful woman that set her off, but this woman just rubbed her all wrong. The sooner Sam could get away, the better she would feel.

"I'll take you home, miss. There is no reason for you to pay a cabbie. I need to run into the supermarket for a few items as it is and I will dispatch you as well."

Sam looked at the man. She thought it was cute the way he was always so prim and proper. She knew somehow that it was not out of character for him to speak this way and she thought that if he was okay with dispatching her, then she was fine with it as well.

Ten minutes later, Sam and Duncan were on their way. He had leant her his cell phone to make a call and had also provided her with the phone number to the pack house so she could make arrangement to get her gear.

"I'm supposed to meet Lieutenant Wolff at the shop tomorrow and he'll give me back my gun and ammo. I guess that's the best I can hope for under the circumstances. Thanks for taking me home, Mr. Duncan."

"You are very welcome, miss. It is my pleasure." He looked like he wanted to say more so Sam waited. "Miss, if you don't mind my asking, what sort of gear, err gun do you carry?"

"It's just Sam, not miss anything. I carry a modified Glock forty with a silencer, fifteen in the magazine with one in the chamber, plus three extra clips. I have been known to carry thirty-eight chiefs special as well, but I like the weight and balance of the Glock better. It's also easier to clean and load. They make the handle small enough for my small hand and I can reload it in the dark."

He had asked, she thought. She was also sure he didn't have a clue what she was talking about. After she had said the word "modified," she had lost him. She wished that she could show him what she meant, but actually was not sure if that would confuse him more or make him more leery of her. She decided that if she ever saw him again, she would make sure to show him her weapon. Everyone needed to have a healthy respect for guns, and a working knowledge if they were ever around one.

Duncan dropped Sam off in front of the bakery twenty minutes later. After his refusal of gas money he drove off. She was able to persuade him to return the next afternoon and pick up some fresh baked goods for all his trouble. Sam figured it was the least she could do under the circumstances.

CHAPTER FIVE

Tucker had watched Sam leave the mansion with Duncan and followed them to the bakery. Tucker didn't let her see him, but he had needed to make sure she got home safely. He stood outside the store front for three hours waiting to see if she left again, and if she did, who with.

Tucker James was a very old vampire, having been turned when he was twenty-six in the year twelve-fourteen, and in over eight hundred years, he had done many things he was not proud of and had seen many things that he wished that he hadn't. But the woman in the building across from him at this moment was the most terrifying thing he had ever encountered. All because he didn't have a clue what to do with her or how to live without her now that he had given her his blood.

He knew that he couldn't mate with her, with anyone as a matter of fact. Tucker had a mistress, his maker. The woman had ruled his life since she turned him, without mercy or love. She'd been telling him that she owned him, and that he would never escape her unless she allowed it. She was cruel and unforgiving. When she found him again, and he had no doubt that she would, he would pay the price for trying to escape her again. Marta Lipscomb was a horror and a whore. She was what nightmares based their horrific cues off of. And he would die the death of his kind before going back to her again.

Oh, she was pretty enough, Tucker supposed. She was plump in a way that said she had had money before she became vampire, enough of it to have kept her well fed and pampered. She was not much older than Tucker, maybe fifty years at the most—not all that many to a vampire, who measured their lives in centuries and lifetimes. But she was as different as day and night to him when it came to their personalities.

While Marta was domineering and cruel, Tucker was quiet and reserved. He would and could sit for hours just watching and listening to the things going on around him. Watch the people of the night flow around him, observing them without interfering. She was flighty and loud, often relying on others to entertain her rather than trying to amuse herself. If left on her own for too long, she would stir up or start something heinous then sit back and watch the bloody outcome, literally.

When Marta was in the mood for sex, which was several times a day, the only way she could climax was to torture and maim with beatings and bloodbaths and days without release for her partners. And no matter what the gender or sexual preference, if they found their release before she let them, she would suck them nearly dry of blood and leave them to live or die in a cell until she forgot them, or they finally succumbed to death. How it ended for them, she didn't care. Any time she wanted sex, it was the same, only the people had changed over time. Her cruelty knew no limits and he'd finally had enough.

This was his last attempt to get away. Tucker had already decided that if he didn't succeed this time, he would walk into the sun. He simply couldn't take it anymore. Eight hundred years was truly enough, more than enough. And now this had happened. A woman he would give anything to have yet couldn't touch.

Tucker had thought to talk with Aaron, to apply for his release on Aaron's behalf. Everyone had heard about how he had saved Dominic Marshall from the same sort of fate, bringing his friend Colin Larimore in and standing by while he had challenged the old master. His defeating him and becoming the master of that realm hadn't just saved Dominic, but all of the vampires of that realm from certain death and starvation. Both Colin and Aaron were men to trust, men to be loyal to.

But Tucker knew that he couldn't do it now. He needed to get away from Sam and all that she would mean to him. If Marta was to find him, and again, of that there was no doubt, Marta would kill him and his true mate and anyone who dared defy her or get in her way. He couldn't let that happen to her.

When Tucker saw a light go on above the little shop, then go off again an hour later, he waited before crossing the street to her shop. He couldn't help himself; he needed to see her again. Tucker moved through the door without any problems. Then moved into the apartment above the same way—by magic. He knew the way; her scent called to him. Her blood called to his. As his mate there were no boundaries.

Sam was sleeping soundly. Tucker's breath caught at the vision before him. She was naked, bared to the moonlight spilling over every inch of her lush body. He touched her gently with his mind and hit the wall she had erected around herself. When he pushed a little harder, she stirred slightly in her sleep. He backed out and stared down at her. She was lovelier than he had ever thought her to be.

Her left breast was exposed and even though he knew he would regret it, Tucker leaned down and licked her nipple then blew a soft, warm breath across it. Her nipple puckered and her breast tightened immediately. It was a tantalizing sight and one he couldn't resist. He wasn't even sure he wanted to. He wanted one more taste, he thought, just once more small taste.

He bent lower and pulled the pebble-sized delight into his mouth, suckling gently at first then harder when she moaned quietly and arched up toward him. He pulled away, knowing that it was much too late now to stop. He needed to have a taste of her. Moving her legs apart gently, he moved between them and touched her nether lips once, twice, until finally, he pushed his long finger inside of her. Both of them moaned at the sensations. The tightness of her nearly made him want to wake her for more, so much more. As he moved his fingers inside of her, he watched her body respond to his movements and hoped that she wouldn't wake up. His need for release was making him take chances that he would never do normally. Instead of leaving like he should have, he reached down with his free hand, unsnapped his pants, and pulled the zipper tab down. His cock, stiff and achy, sprang forward into his fist. He moved his fist up and down his shaft in time with the movement of his finger. As he felt her wetness soaking his hand, he pushed two, then three fingers in her wet heat, her body moving with him, undulating and pushing against him, her sheath milking his fingers like he imaged her doing to his cock. Their moans filled the small bedroom, his deeper, hers a sensual concert over his already fevered body.

His body was ready to explode, so close he knew he may come at any second, and he could feel her release was close too, and smell it on her. He needed to taste her creamy essences, her spicy juices overwhelming. Just a taste, he promised himself, and leaned down to take her pussy into his mouth. He licked hard against her clit, gathering as much of her cream as he could on his tongue, and drank, lapping more and more into him and down his throat. As she jerked up into a hard release a loud scream, Tucker came as well. His cum jettisoned onto his shirt and hand as he continued to taste her until the last tremor died away.

With her climax, her scent, her special smell for him, strengthened by her release. It poured into him. He could smell the peaches and cream as though they were spread out before him just as she was. With a final lap of her juices on her thighs, he leaned his head against the mattress for a few minutes, trying to catch his breath.

Tucker had never meant to take her like that. What he had done was akin to rape and he knew then that he had been no better than Marta when it came to taking what she had wanted. He felt guilty about it, felt as if he had betrayed her with what he had done. He promised himself that he would make it up to her. Tucker raised his head to see if she still slept and looked right into her beautiful eyes.

He didn't move, didn't even so much as breathe. When she turned her head on a heavy sigh, closing her eyes as she went, he pulled the shadows around himself and dematerialized from her room before it was too late. He was nearly to his lair when he thought maybe he was already too late.

~~~

Sam was downstairs the next morning when Betty and Sally showed up at five-thirty. Their voices and general moving around while they came in the back door together sounded like a herd of elephants and a bunch of chattering monkeys. She wondered if the two of them ever did anything quietly, then she smiled. She sincerely doubted it.

Sam hadn't slept well after she woke sometime after four this morning and had gotten up to sit on the window seat and watch the street start to wake. She wondered about the man in her dream, a very erotic wet dream. She couldn't shake the feeling of near complete satisfaction and wasn't sure she wanted to. Her body was relaxed from the orgasm, but she was still tense and on edge. As if she hadn't gotten enough of whatever had made her climax like that. She blushed at how hard she had come and how much the man in her dream had seemed so real. She tried to shake off the feeling of connection to him, the overwhelming need to find him. Silly, she thought. Just plain silly.

She showed the women what things to take up front and also let them know where any orders were that were to be picked up this morning. Sam told them that she had a few things to finish up but if they needed her for anything just to shout. She had missed working a full day yesterday and the day before and needed to make up for it. The timer went off for another tray of baked goods and she pulled them out to cool.

Sam was decorating a layer cake with pink roses when the hair on the back of her neck stood up. She put down the tube of pink frosting and went to the one-way mirror that looked into the main part of the shop. Something was...wrong. Someone was in a great deal of pain, both mentally and physically. She watched the people standing there waiting for their treats and baked goods, reached out to them, and found the one she was looking for. There, she thought, the woman in the blue top and spandex pants. She looked frightened. Then she realized it was terror the woman was feeling—terror and pain, immense pain. This woman was being beaten by someone close to her and quite frequently too.

Settling deeper into her mind, Sam could feel the woman's pain and she took a quick inventory of her injuries. She had six bruised ribs and one broken one. Her jaw was also bruised and hurting, but she had tried to cover it with a good amount of makeup. Whoever the beater was had snatched this woman's hair at one point and she had a large raw place on her scalp from it. Sam was sure that blood scabbed in the area and the woman was terrified that someone might notice. Blue top, as Sam called her in her mind, was wearing long sleeves and a sweater to cover the hand prints left there around her biceps. She was nervous and terrified. The heat and weather alone would be enough to alert most that she was hiding something.

Sam touched her mind deeper still. She wasn't surprised what she saw there. The woman was going to kill herself when she returned home. Just a simple as that, something she had added to her list of things to do — make the beds, do the dishes, fold laundry, put gun to head, and pull the trigger. Of course this was after she saw that her husband's meal was cooked perfectly for him and the whole house was spic and span. Anger surged through Sam, hot and sharp.

Sam planted the urge for Blue-Top to call Sam before she made the beds. She would need to call not just think about it. When she got home, she was to go directly to the phone and call. Sam then gave her the phone number of the cell phone that no one knew about but a very select group of people. There were no small children involved. The woman had a son, but he had long since written his mom off, the woman thought. Sam wondered fleetingly if the son was like that father. But dismissed it almost immediately. That, Sam thought, was not her concern. Satisfied, Sam went back to work on the pink frosted cake.

Sam had been helping people for nearly ten years. And contrary to popular belief, not all abused spouses were women. There were a great many men as well; women were just as mean as men when they wanted to be. While Sam didn't have any direct contact with the underground system she used, she knew all of the participants by first name and voice. No one had been caught in all the time she had been a part of it and Sam never took risks with either the people she helped out of terrible situations, or the people she relied on to make it possible. Once they entered the system, they never made contact with anyone again. Their lives officially ended the day that Sam or one of the others got them out. Sam liked it that way.

She finished the cake she was working on and concentrated on the perfection of each tiny flower as she created it, not the job she was to do later. After it was boxed up and tagged, she went to tell Sally that she had an assignment tonight and to close up for her. Lieutenant Wolff was going to be there in half an hour to bring her the weapon and ammo he had taken for safe keeping. She wanted to be completely ready to go when he left. He was a typical male wolf when he finally showed up.

"This is a big gun for a woman, Sam, don't you think? I don't mean that you can't handle it. Nope, not what I mean at all. In fact, I've no doubt that you are likely a better shot than me. But I would like to know what are you doing with it?" He wasn't even trying to be clever about asking.

Sam knew that David was a good cop. Just like she knew he was a were. Recently, she had heard that his brother was the alpha of the pack in this area too. And she figured that he had already run ballistics on the weapon. She didn't care; she knew that it would come up clean. All her weapons would. She got rid of the ones she used by ways that no one would ever find them.

"There is also some gun powder residue on it. Want to explain why that is? I know it's not from yesterday. You said yourself you didn't fire your weapon. Sara and Shade said the only shot had come from Andrew Ship's gun."

Raising her brow at this tone, she decided to try and skirt around him. "Is there a problem with my permit, Lieutenant?" When in doubt, answer with a question. It was better to have them frustrated than to give away information she hadn't meant to. She also knew she had never used this particular gun for anything other than target practice anyway.

"No, there isn't a problem. I know you're not stupid and you probably know your rights as well as anyone. If there was a problem, Sam, we'd be having this conversation at the station house and not here. Are you planning on having one anytime soon—a problem I mean?"

Sam grinned at him. He really was a good guy, she thought. "I don't generally make plans that involve using a gun, sir. Unless it's at the range. That would be just plain stupid, don't you think?" She grinned when he frowned at her. "I have it for safety reasons. We make deposits here every day and the three of us are all women. You wouldn't want us to not be able to protect ourselves, would you? I do, however, know how to use any and all guns I have ever used. Just like you do, I'm sure."

"It's not 'sir,' it's David, just David. And I don't make plans either, but sometimes things just happen." He looked frustrated. And if he paced any harder, she was sure he would wear a nice path in the concrete long before it would wear from regular use. "Well?"

She looked at him, confused; he hadn't asked her a question, so she was not sure what he meant. She shrugged. "Well, what, sir, I mean, David?"

"Did anything happen?"

Sam wanted to laugh at his question, but thought it might be wiser to just have some fun for a bit. At least until he pissed her off. "When?" She tried to look innocent, but she couldn't quite pull it off. Probably, she thought, because she was having a hard time controlling her laughter.

"With the gun, why you carry it. Did anything happen?" His voice took on a tone she was used to. A tone of someone who wanted answers but didn't want to cause trouble to someone he liked. And she could sense that David did like her. Like her even though he thought of her as a pain in the ass.

"To the gun? Why would anything happen to the gun?" She was really trying to keep it light, to diffuse and confuse. She didn't want to hurt David's feelings, she liked, and well…she respected him too much. But that didn't mean she couldn't have some fun too.

"What?" He looked at her as he asked. Snapped would have been a better term, but it was still a good question.

"Huh?"

She just knew that this could go on for hours if she let it. She was sure whatever had been his original concern was now lost. As he rubbed his forehead between his eyes, she tried to hide a smile. He was getting a headache and it was her fault, she was sure. He was clearly at his end of patience when he snapped at her.

"Have you killed anyone with this gun, Sam? Or shot anyone, or done anything that I should know about?"

"No, si...no, I haven't shot or killed anyone with that gun. Nor have I done anything you should be aware of involving this gun."

He looked at her skeptically. She had worded it just as he had asked her about the gun. She could tell that he was trying to figure her out and that he was not sure right now about her strange answers. But he would figure it out, she was sure. She just hoped he did long after she had completed her assignment for the night.

David left the shop ten minutes later, no closer to understanding her need for the handgun than before he started talking to her. She noticed that David was pulling out his cell phone as he exited the building. She didn't have time to try and figure out what he was doing. Mrs. Blue-Top, Elizabeth Siemens, was waiting for her.

Sam left the shop at four o'clock and headed to Mrs. Siemens' house. Bethany had called just as she was supposed to and was right now gathering up a few personal belongings to take with her when she left. Sam planned to get to the house by four-thirty and was going into the house through the back of the garage, just as the two women had planned.

Sam felt the first tingle of magic when she got out of her car. She looked around the street where she was parked and didn't see anything out of the ordinary. She locked up and started down the street. She opened herself up to find what her other senses couldn't.

She didn't like reaching out while she was on an assignment, but she was nervous after the Ship incident. She felt the first man about three blocks back on the opposite side of the street walking in the same direction she was. He was a wolf, pack wolf. The other one was also a wolf and was in front of her about two blocks on the same side of the street but walking toward her. She knew that they were only to follow her and not to harm nor to intercede. She also knew who had sent them. She could live with that, almost.

David and his brother Bradley had assigned them to her. She didn't need or want a keeper and it pissed her off to no end to think that they thought she did. Sam had been taking care of herself for a long time and she wasn't about to have an overgrown dog try to do so now. Especially when she had done nothing to warrant it.

The first man dropped to the ground in mid-step. He was asleep before his head hit the hard ground. She could have had him drop slowly, but was too mad to worry about niceties. The second man was a little more difficult as he was in a shop district and having him just drop might cause a ruckus. She laughed out loud when she thought how to take care of him. She gave him this sudden and overwhelming urge to use the bathroom—like right friggin' now! And felt the moment his attention was elsewhere. She would never humiliate anyone, so it was only an urge and not actually anything major. She was still smiling when she stepped into Bethany Siemen's garage.

Beth, as she asked to be called, was so grateful to Sam that she didn't think they were going to ever make it to the car. They had had to stop every ten feet so that Beth could hug Sam again. Normally not one to let people hug her, she felt this woman needed the soft physical contact more than Sam needed to make her stop doing it. It took them nearly twenty minutes to make what would normally be a three minute walk.

When Beth asked if she could stop at the bank and take out some funds, Sam had explained that if Beth didn't normally do this, then the bank clerk may alert Beth's husband that she was there. Beth didn't know if her name was even on the account. Sam made a few calls and found that not only was Beth's name not on the account, but that if she used any of the household money or credit cards that the bank was to notify Mr. Siemens soon, if not immediately.

The bank assistant, a Tally Marsh, was a good friend to Mrs. Siemens' grown daughter. And Sam also knew from her own dealings with the bank that Tally was a wolf — one of the few Sam trusted. Tally told Sam that if she would bring Beth in and her driver's license, Tally would see what she could do for the woman. Tally apparently knew a little about the situation at the Siemens home and would do everything she could to help out.

Forty-five minutes later, Beth was nearly eight hundred dollars richer and on her way to a better life. She had tried several times to give Sam money, but Sam kept refusing her.

"This isn't why I do this, and paying me isn't an option. You keep your money, Beth. You are going to have to start a new life and money may be tight for a while. The people you are meeting will be very helpful and will do anything to keep you safe. Listen to them and you'll be safe. I promise."

With tears in her eyes, Beth got out of the car and onto the second of many parts of her safe journey far away from an abusive husband. Some of the women they saved went back to the men who abused them, she knew this. But she couldn't make them keep safe anymore than she could control the weather. That's just the way it was. Some people didn't understand or know any other way of life.

Sam parked her car in the private garage and got into her little sedan that she had parked just down the street. She loved to drive, and she did it very fast. Too fast for those who rode with her sometimes. And when she was upset or pissed as she was right now, she also drove a little recklessly.

Her first stop was to the station house. She asked to see David Wolff and was granted permission from the large man at the desk to go back to his office. He was never too busy for a pretty girl, the Entry Control Chief told her; no one should ever be that. She thanked him politely and went back. The moment he stepped around his desk to greet her, she drew back and slugged him square in the nose, slamming his body against the desk and knocking him to the floor. David wisely stayed where he was.

"You set your watch dogs on me again and I will use my gun for things you will be very aware of. I don't want, don't need, nor do I require your help. Do I make myself clear?"

"Crystal. But it was..." He shut up the moment her foot lifted off the floor and swung back as though to kick him in the head.

"I will hurt you. You had no right to send pack members to follow me. You do not own me, nor do I answer to you. Do it again and I will not be content to just put them out of commission for a few hours." He fell into a deep sleep as soon as she touched his forehead.

A few minutes later, nursing a bruised hand, she stormed out of the station house. Next, she went to the pack house. Going to the top sometimes got one better results than going through the middle man. And Sam wanted results. The longer it took her to get there, the more pissed off she became. By the time she was racing up the drive, she was ready to shoot any and all the men she had to deal with.

When she arrived at the pack house, Bradley was on the front porch. Good, she thought. He looked as if he hadn't a care in the world. She sat in her car for a minute trying to regain control of her temper and finally said fuck it. He was going to get it with both barrels. He had been forewarned by David after he woke up, Sam figured.

~~~

Bradley was casually leaning again one of the posts with his hands in his pockets. His men had returned just under an hour ago, embarrassed and mad. He didn't blame them; it really hurt to be bested by a woman, especially one as beautiful as this. Bradley put out his hand to her, smile on his face when she stepped out of the car.

"Miss Hunter. How nice of you to join us. I hope you'll be staying for supper. You'd be surprised at the way the cook feeds us." Bradley had to smile. She was fuming, he could see that from where he stood, and if that was in doubt, her next sentence left no doubt whatsoever.

"You mother fucking, cock sucking son of a bitch. If you ever, and I do mean ever, send someone to tag me again, I will personally come here and blow your fucking nuts off. I have never been so angry in my entire life! What do you think would have happened if her husband had come home and found Tweedle Dee and Tweedle Dumb there? Do you think it's easy to get an abused woman..." She slapped her hand over her mouth and stared at him with her eyes wide open.

"Do go on. Please don't stop now. It was just getting interesting." He leaned back against the house. "You were saying how you rescued an abused woman today. I'm sure your mate would want to know about that as well. How you go into houses and help these women out, help them pack up their memories. What do you do when the husband shows up? Ah, the gun. Now I understand."

Bradley could smell the vampire all over Sam, and he also knew that the vampire was close to her, but not as close Bradley was. He started advancing toward her, to do what he wasn't sure. Shaking some sense into her head came to mind. Then he stopped suddenly when she pulled out the Glock and pointed it at his chest. *Shit!*

Her hand was steady and straight. Bradley figured she knew how to use it and wouldn't be the least bit hesitant about doing so. He knew from talking to David that she had one in the chamber, and quite a few extra clips. Bradley took a few steps back. He had stupidly thought he could handle one little human and had sent his bodyguard in the house. If she shot him—no, when she shot him, he knew he would be dead long before anyone would be able to rescue him. He raised his hands up and faced his palms out.

"Don't do it, Sam. I...David and I just wanted to make sure you weren't doing anything stupid." Her look made him very nervous. "Not that you're stupid, but things could get out of hand, especially with guns."

He took two steps back until his heel hit the bottom step of the porch he had stepped off of. He was not going to give her any reason to put a bullet in his head. He could smell the silver and cursed his own stupidity once again.

"Do I look like I can't handle a gun, alpha? Don't take another step or I will shoot you, have no doubt. Right now I'm mad enough to shoot you just to watch you bleed. I don't think I've ever been this mad before." She took one step toward him. "What the fuck were you thinking, if you were at all? That the little woman couldn't possibly survive without the big bad man to save her? I don't need your fucking help."

"I can see that now. I'm not moving, Sam. Please don't shoot me. You know as well as I do that you won't get away. There are several hundred pack members that will track you down in minutes." He hoped that wouldn't be necessary. He really wanted to live. But he was partly responsible for pissing her off.

"Threatening me right now isn't conducive to calming me down, asshole. And if I shoot you, no matter how many pack members come after me, you'll still be a dead dog."

He decided now was probably not the time to point out he wasn't dog, but wolf. "All right, you're right. I apologize. What can I do to reassure that we are all friends here?"

Her snort was not making him feel warm and fuzzy.

Bradley reached out and found the vamp about a hundred yards to the West. He sent him a plea to come and calm his mate. His reply from him was anything but helpful. Bradley wished like hell he'd never heard of the woman in front of him.

"She isn't aware of me, not as her mate, nor as a man. I can't make myself known to her without bringing harm to her. I have contacted Aaron, the master of this realm, and he is on his way. Hold steady until he is able to get there."

"How can she not be aware of you? I can smell you all over her." Bradley was going to stake the bastard. "And what do you mean she isn't aware of you as a man? You do realize she has a gun pointed at me and the shot is silver. I'm not too terribly fond of dying right now. Get your ass over here and defuse the situation."

"Hold steady, he is nearly here."

Tucker was closer to her now too. Only about ten feet away, Bradley estimated, but it didn't help him if she shot. Tucker would take her out of harm's way if needed, but nothing more than that, Bradley knew. It was the way of mates. You couldn't do anything but protect them no matter how pissed off you knew it was going to make them. He just hoped he got the opportunity to do that with his own mate someday. Bradley could feel Aaron's presence immediately after he entered his territory. Christ, he was never doing this again.

~~~

Aaron appeared next to Tucker and pulled the shadows around himself just as Tucker had done. Aaron had been

61

about to make love to his lovely mate when Tucker had told him he was in serious trouble and needed him to please come to the pack house. Thinking Bradley was hurt or worse, he'd left immediately. Tucker had told him that Sam, the woman from his home, was going to shoot the alpha for reasons he didn't know.

"I know that you have claimed her. So why am I here?" Aaron demanded of the vamp.

He, too, could smell the vamp on the girl. Her scent was stronger with her anger. Tucker should have been able to take control as soon as it had gotten out of hand.

"I haven't made myself known to her. She isn't aware of me, nor have I marked or mated with her, just bonded." Tucker dropped his chin to his chest and then he dropped to the ground.

Aaron was furious. He didn't want his people to be afraid of him, but he also needed them to respect the rules of the realm. If Tucker wanted to stay under his protection, then he was going to have to know that while Aaron demanded respect, he also gave it. Aaron reached out, took the man's chin in his hand, and lifted it to look him in the eyes. He looked deep into them, seeing the man he could be.

"This is my realm and as such, my will is law. Do you understand me? You will come back to the mansion with me as soon as this is complete. I will not be put off in this. If you do not show, Tucker James, I will consider it a breach of contract and have you hunted down like an animal. Do you understand all that I have ordered this day?"

Aaron hated making it a demand, but this man was hurting and in need of something desperately. Aaron could smell Sam on Tucker, and it was more than the healing feed he had given her a few days ago. He had had sex with her and that was as bonding as it got.

"Yes, my lord. I will come with you as soon as you make her safe. She...she is very angry and though you smell her around me, she isn't aware...I took advantage of her while she slept. I didn't harm her, but I took what was not offered from her."

Aaron didn't understand that statement, but knew that he needed to rescue the alpha first. "I see. Actually, no I don't, but you will explain yourself to me and to her. I will do my best with your mate, Tucker, but as I have had very little to do with this woman, I'm not sure how to handle her. But I can assure you that according to my mate, keeping her safe and out of jail will be a full time job. And not one I'm willing to help you with every day."

Aaron walked up a few steps past the girl and stopped halfway between her and Bradley. Aaron felt her track him with her eyes and he was surprised by that. When shadowed as he'd been, humans were not able to see him. He materialized when he was standing between her and the alpha.

"Miss Hunter, always a pleasure to meet the new people in my realm. I understand that you and our esteemed alpha have had some issues today. Perhaps I can be of some assistance."

Sam simply reached behind her and pulled out another Glock that she'd had hidden there. Before Aaron could blink, she had this one pointed at him. Aaron moved only to raise his hands up in much the same way that Bradley had done. The situation had just gone from bad to worst. Well, fuck.

"Oh, yeah, that's helpful," Bradley snarled from behind him. "Now she had two targets instead of one. Remind me again why you're the bad-ass Master of the Realm." Aaron growled at Bradley and almost laughed when he growled right back. This was so not amusing.

"Just so you both know, I'm a dead shot at any distance. I can and have taken out a man's Adams Apple at seventy-five feet, centering six bullets point blank. That was using my left hand. My right is just as good, only I missed one and it hit him between the eyes. Bad shot, I guess, but only in making him die quickly." She shrugged; Aaron shuddered. He didn't think she was kidding. "I know that neither of you are human, not that I really give a rat's ass, but these are silver shots. You, bloodsucker guy, you can help me by backing the fuck up. The dog and I are having a private conversation here and you were not invited."

Aaron wanted to. He wanted to go home and go back to making love to his mate. But before he could say anything, Bradley growled again.

"I'm not a fucking dog, damn it. You know, I think you need someone to paddle that ass of yours. I'm sick to death of this bull shit. Why the fuck am I even a target in this? Because I tried to protect you?"

"Bradley, let's not piss her off any more than she apparently is." Aaron was going to die, he just knew it. "Remember, she does have a gun on us both. Tucker, I think this would be a good time to make yourself known to your mate."

Aaron was a little nervous, but trying hard not to show it. Sam was not. All he could smell on her was Tucker and pissed off female. He could feel that she would shoot either or both of them without any problems or much more provocation. He wasn't even sure what the hell had happened in the first place. And on top of that, he was going to have to punish the both of them. If he lived...he surely hoped that he would.

Tucker was suddenly in front of Sam. She didn't even back up and didn't seem to be afraid of him, which surprised him. They stared at each other for all of ten seconds before she turned and aimed both guns at his chest. He reached out and touched her forehead, said "sleep," and caught her as she tumbled into his arms. Aaron took the first deep breath he'd had since coming here. And he used it to snarl at the vampire who held the young woman in his arms.

CHAPTER SIX

Sam woke up in the same damned bedroom she had been in before. Frustrated at ending up in this house again so soon after leaving made her want to punch someone, hard. So, kicking violently at the blankets, she threw herself out of bed and right into the arms of the man who had stood in front of her at the alpha's house. Her first thought was that he was incredibly tall. Then she could smell him. She barely caught herself before she leaned in and buried her nose in his neck.

"You. Don't you dare you touch me! What the hell...let me go you...you dickhead!" Embarrassment notched up her anger a little higher than it would normally have been.

She struggled to get away for few more minutes, and then collapsed against him. As soon as he loosened his grip, she jerked her knee up, narrowly missing his balls. As he went to grab for her again before she hurt him or herself, she elbowed him in the ribs. As he clutched the bruised area, she snapped her head back and slammed it into his nose.

"Stop right now," he roared. "Christ, woman, what's wrong with you?"

He was holding his nose with one hand and his ribs with the other. She took a step back. If he touched her again, she was going to claw his eyes out. Then maybe she'd smell him again.

"I want you to move out of my way. I don't have any idea how I keep ending up at this house, but I damned well am going home." She started for the door and stopped. "Wait a minute—you did it, didn't you? How did you do that? You put me under somehow." She remembered something else. He was near her in the dark, and she frowned at him, trying to place it.

"Yes. I put you in a deep sleep." He grinned and her heart flipped over. "I thought it was deeper than this, that you'd still be sleeping right now. I have to go to see the master of this realm and I don't want you to leave yet. I would like to talk to you. Will you be all right if I leave you alone for a while?"

"I'm not staying here. If you think that, then you're nuttier than a fruit cake." She started for the door again only to be blocked by him. "I have things to get finished before I open tomorrow and hanging out with this family isn't high on my list of fun things to do. You and I have nothing to say to each other."

Sam turned to find her pants. Both times she had ended up in this flipping house. And it seemed that she would end up without her clothes. They seemed to just disappear. And her friggin' guns. Damn it, if she had to go through that wolf again to get them, she would just buy another one. Well, when she could get six hundred bucks together that was. She leaned down on her knees to see if they had fallen under the bed and heard the man behind her groan.

When she turned around, Tucker was still staring at her ass. He took his time, sliding his eyes from her ass to her breasts then finally up to her face. He grinned at her.

"Enjoying yourself there, fang face?" Normally, she would have pulled her shirt down over her bare butt, but she didn't seem to mind that he was looking, and that made her pissy too.

"Yes. Yes, I am." He grinned again. "I want you very badly. I ache with need for you."

Her heart stuttered several beats. She sat back on her heels and scrambled back, then more when he advanced toward her, slow and determined. Sam continued to back up until she hit the wall behind her, but he kept walking. She began to crawl up the wall until she was standing. He stopped when he was just inches from her.

"You...you need to...this isn't going to happen, you know. I don't...I...we aren't...back up, please?"

Her voice was huskier, deeper than before. And her body felt heavier, needy with...she was not sure for what, but knew that he would have it. The problem was she wasn't sure whether she wanted him to back away or not. But he was close. Close enough for her to want to sniff at him again. She looked up into his eyes and she groaned this time.

Tucker was a very handsome man, beautiful in fact. His hair was long on the upper half of his head, and hung nearly to his waist. He had it tied with a leather strip at the back of his neck. The bottom portion of his head was shaved close with fine stubble of dark hair, darker than the top, which was a deep mahogany that had been shined to a glossy shine. His face was a classic one, fine bone structure, high cheek bones, and dark, smooth brows over eyes a starling shade of dark blue. His nose had been broken before. She could see where it had healed incorrectly, leaving a small knot in the middle of the long slope that added to his looks rather than took away from them. His jaw was jutted and strong-looking. She found herself wanting to bite it, just a nibble or two. Tucker's shoulders were wide and well defined, biceps that measured at least twenty-two inches, she guessed. He had a tall, lean figure, six-foot-four at the very least. His chest was wide and Sam would bet were muscled along with abs that were washboard rippled and hard as rock. Sam doubted the man had an ounce of fat on him.

~~~

"Why? Don't you want me to touch you, Sam? I can smell you, your heat, and your need. I don't want to stop. I don't think you do either, do you?" He touched her cheek, and watched with fascination as her eyes deepened to a deeper violet. Tucker slowly raised his other hand to her hip and pulled her body to his. He lowered his head to hers. "Sam..."

"Daddy said to come down now. That it's time to pay the piper." Mac's high-pitched voice cut through them as if he had used a rapier.

Tucker backed up immediately, dropping his hands from her. But not before he saw her flare of disappointment. Sam turned away from him. Closing his eyes, Tucker tried to get his body under control before he turned to the boy in the doorway.

"I need to go down now. I need to talk with the master as he's commanded. You must stay here and wait for me."

Tucker wanted to pull her back into his arms, just to hold her, to pick her up and cradle her. He was surprised by this need. He wasn't much of a touchy person. He felt her shame and embarrassment, and he wanted to soothe her, but didn't have any idea how to do that to someone.

"Go. Just leave me alone." Tucker watched as Sam walked into the bathroom and quietly closed the door behind her. When he started toward the bathroom, he stopped when he heard the lock turn.

"Are you coming? Dad said to come on down when you're ready, but not to take too long," Mac said and turned and left. With another look toward the bathroom door,

Tucker left. He would talk to her when he returned — if he returned.

"Master, mistress. I beg entrance please?" Tucker had been taught, and none too gently, to never go anywhere or into any room he was not specifically invited to. The repercussions of a mistake like that would stay with him for days, if not weeks. And once learned, he didn't soon forget.

Tucker had once, in the very beginning of his life as a vampire, walked into the room he had been assigned. He had been a vampire maybe about fifteen years. It hadn't occurred to him that the room wasn't his to do with as he pleased. He had simply walked into a bedroom he had been sleeping in forever and always without asking for permission. And calling it a bedroom was really giving much more credit for the room than it deserved, as it was no more than a rag on the dirt floor of a four-by-four foot cell. Mistress was there waiting for him, just to catch him making a mistake, he was sure.

She had ordered him on his knees first and when the first slice of the whip bit into his skin, he nearly cried out from it. The whip had been specially made for her, she had told him once. There were at least a dozen long strips of leather, each one with several barbs of silver wrapped around them. He had taken only thirty lashes that night, more than he had ever received to that point, but not the most he would feel against his back in his long servitude with her. Pain riddled his body and he knew when she finished with the whip, she wasn't finished with him yet.

When she had ordered him to stand, he knew, just knew, he had to leave her. He had to get away before it was too late.

Moving slowly, pain rippling through his back, he stood with his hand behind him and his head bowed. Mistress had ordered one of the other guards to stand behind him and remove his clothes. Once he was naked, she dropped before Tucker and started to fondle his balls none too gently. He knew that he couldn't say anything, nor could he pull back from the pain. His body was used to her abuse and his cock lay limp in her hands. He hoped he could remain that way for all of eternity if necessary.

But when she took him into her mouth, he hardened immediately and grew harder still as she sucked and licked. Holding back a groan and his climax, he closed his eyes to the sensation. Suddenly, she bit him—she had bit into his cock deep and painfully. As she began sucking from the blood from it, nearly draining him dry, he felt his knees shake and tremble. When she had finished, he dropped to the floor and couldn't move. Since that night, he couldn't stand for her to touch him, not that it had stopped her, but to have her bite such a sensitive part of him nearly ended him.

"Come in, Tucker," the master's mate said, bringing him back to the present. "And in this house it isn't necessary to ask to enter a room."

She didn't understand that he couldn't go against centuries of training. He was bigger than the master, in frame and height. But his subservient ways made her nervous, he knew. But he could no more stop being that way than he could stop drinking blood.

"Yes, mistress." Tucker bowed his head, not making eye contact with anyone in the room as he entered. He didn't need to look around to know where they both were. The mistress was near the chair that the master was sitting in. The chair was just to the right of the fireplace.

"Have a seat on the sofa there, Tucker. I want to get to know you and why you have decided to forgo asking to be a part of this realm. And then we'll talk about your relationship with Sam." Startled for a second, Tucker looked up quickly when Aaron spoke. His voice had been soft and kind.

"We don't have a relationship, so there isn't anything to talk to him about. And in the future, I can speak for myself." Sam barreled into the room like a bull as she thought to correct the master. Tucker felt a smile spread across his face. He should have known that she wouldn't stay in the background. It just was not in her nature.

"Ah, Miss Hunter. Since you have decided to be a part of this conversation, would you care to have a seat as well?" Aaron pointed to the couch where Tucker sat. "You and I have much to talk about also, I think. And as for your lack of relationship with Tucker, we'll see, won't we?"

"I want my guns. I'm getting sick of waking up here without them. And then I am leaving this mad house." Sam turned to glare at Lizzy. "If you do not stop poking at me, I'm going to give you something to think about next time you try."

"Don't you dare threaten my daughter, you half-wit. I'll have you know that she is just a child and doesn't know what she is doing. So back off or find I'm not so easy to intimidate as a child," Sara roared as she came up off the couch. Tucker found himself standing in front of Sam quicker than he thought he could move.

"Gladly," Sam snarled from behind him.

In the next second, Sara dropped to the floor, her hands gripping her head tightly. Blood poured from her nose and ears. She groaned on the floor in apparent agony. Sara screamed and screamed while holding her head. Magic rippled in the room as several people shimmered like falling rain into the room. Tucker backed closer to his mate to protect her.

"Stop it right now," Aaron screamed as he flashed forward to go to his own mate's rescue, which would have been toward Sam.

But Tucker was closer. Tucker slammed his considerable body weight into Aaron seconds before he could touch her, Tucker's instinct kicking in to protect his mate.

Suddenly, Sam was picked up and thrown hard against the wall. Tucker heard her head hit hard, and knew she would be unconscious before she slumped to the floor. He nearly went to her when a command stilled the room instantly.

"Stop! You, all of you, sit down! Aaron! See to Sara." The being pointed at Tucker. "You, young man, see to that woman over there. Oh, no you don't, young lady. Lizzy, you come back here right now and sit down."

The older woman took command at once, ordering everyone about to see to the injured. Tucker didn't worry about who they were or how they happened to be there. He was just grateful that he could see to Sam.

"But Grandma, I didn't hurt Mamma." Tucker watched as the older being glared at the child. He didn't know the relationship, but the child sat down and shut up.

"Sit!" This time, the other woman moved toward the center of the room. Tucker was impressed. Pissed, but also impressed at the way they seemed to handle this skirmish as if it were nothing at all.

"Now, Sara, love, are you all right? No, don't try to hurt Sam." She pressed Sara's hand back to her side. "Listen to me. She didn't hurt you—well, not as bad as she could have. Could she, Lizzy? And don't you dare lie to me."

"Now, that is..." Tucker watched as the big master moved to stand in front of the little girl. His eyes had turned and his fangs were deep and long. Tucker pulled Sam into his arms and held her to his chest. He would protect her at all costs.

"Listen to me, Aaron. That poor girl over there, Sam, I believe, only hit Sara with half of what Lizzy has been hitting her with for, well, I would say for several days now." The woman holding Sara's hand glared at the child. "How long, Lizzy?"

"She wouldn't let me in. I couldn't break her door down, so I kept trying harder and harder." Lizzy dropped her head down and quietly said, "Since I met her last week."

"Half? Are you kidding me? Lizzy, you've been digging at her mind for over a week and only half as hard as she hit me? Oh my God, Lizzy, you could have killed her. That should have killed her. She's a human! What were you thinking, young lady?" Sara stood and looked down at the little girl. Tucker stood with Sam in his arms. He'd had enough of this. Besides, it seemed to be a family thing of which neither of them were a part of. Her head wound was bleeding and he wasn't sure what would happen if she wasn't healed again soon.

"Excuse me, sire, mistress. But I would like to take Sam somewhere to rest. Her head is bleeding quite profusely. With your permission, sire, may I retire her to that room again? I believe there I will be able to see to the wound."

Tucker knew there was a tone in his voice. He hoped that with everything going on no one would notice. His mate was hurt and he wanted...no, he needed to heal her.

"I will see to her wound with you, Master Tucker. If you would please follow me, I have gathered the approximate items we will need to close that wound and wrap it up. The poor little mite." Duncan stood next to him with a small chest. Tucker looked again. Yes, a chest.

"I will also make sure that there is plenty of juice for her. She will need to replenish her loss of blood as well. I believe I will need to put money on the stock market in hospital supplies if this continues. We seem to be forever bandaging someone up in this household."

Duncan led Tucker and the bundle in his arms to the same bedroom that Sam had been in twice before now.

While Tucker held Sam, Duncan changed the linens and remade the bed for her. Tucker even held her over the bathroom vanity while Duncan stitched up her head and wrapped tight gauze around it. It was quite a cut, requiring fourteen stitches, but she would be all right in the morning. Tucker would make sure of it. Duncan told him how he'd been bandaging people in this household for years when Tucker had commented on how well the man seemed to be at it.

When Tucker was finally left alone, he lowered Sam gently to the bed. He knew she slept bare, but was not sure he could manage stripping her down without hurting himself sexually in the process. So he took off her jeans, socks, and shoes. He unbuttoned the shirt down far enough to unclasp the front closure on her bra, but left it where it was. He wanted to give her his vein, but didn't want to chance waking her just yet.

He watched her for several minutes before someone came into the room. Tucker didn't look to the person in the doorway, but continued to look at his Sam as he spoke softly. He was loathe to leave her, but knew that he must.

"She is resting now. Mr. Duncan said that her head would hurt in the morning, but otherwise she wouldn't have any ill effects of tonight." Tucker knew the master was standing there. He could also feel his anger.

"I'd like to have a word with you, Tucker," Aaron said just as softly.

"Yes, sire. I will accept my punishment without complaint. I did attack you in your own home. I have no excuse for what I did. I would ask if you could see that Sam is taken care of and protected. I...I know that I shouldn't ask this of you, but she didn't—"

"Come with me, Tucker, please. Let Sam rest without us talking around her. No one will bother her here. She is safe. And Lizzy won't hurt her again either. Her mother and I will see to that."

Tucker reached down and touched her creamy skin, running his finger along the softness and then over her full lips. Then he leaned down and gently touched his lips to hers. He realized at that moment that he had never kissed her mouth before, didn't know what she tasted like there. Well, he thought, it was too late for that now. He started to stand then stopped. Leaning down, he kissed her once more, and whispered against her mouth, "I could have loved you for an eternity."

CHAPTER SEVEN

Aaron walked ahead of Tucker as they went down the long hallway toward Aaron's study. He was still trying to figure the man out. Aaron had never met anyone so beaten before, not just physically, but mentally as well. He had started to do a search on Tucker James. He wanted to try and get a better handle on the man, see where he had come from and why had he stopped here. But something had stopped him from going ahead with it; something told Aaron that it would be a mistake to let anyone know where Tucker was, maybe a fatal one for him. When Tucker was seated across from him, Aaron began.

"First, I want to apologize to you for hurting Sam. I, too, must protect my mate, but what I did was hurt yours without finding out the facts before I reacted. All I could see what that Sara was hurting and nothing more. I'm very sorry for what happened to Sam."

Tucker's head jerked up. The look of surprise was very evident on his face. He had obviously never expected this. Then Aaron watched as the look of fear quickly moved into his eyes. Then he dropped his head again. Something or someone terrified this man.

"Who is it? Who do you hide from, Tucker? Who hurt you so badly that you cower when you enter a room?

Someone has done this to you, and I'd like to know who." Aaron started to stand, but stayed where he was. "You came here seeking my help, did you not? And have decided, for your own reasons, not to ask for it. I would like to know why." Aaron was not a vain man, but he was curious as to why Tucker had decided that Aaron was not worth asking now.

For long moments, not a sound was made; all that could be heard was the ticking of the clock on the desk. Tucker seemed to be trying to make a decision and from the look on his face, a very difficult one. Aaron was relieved when Tucker decided to share his story.

"I'm trying to be free. My maker, she calls to me even now. I wish to escape her, to sever ties, but I can't do that now. I can't risk Sam. I wish that I could stay. We've...we've heard about you helping others, taking them in. It...Marta, she's dangerous and cruel. I fear that when she does find me, she will make me suffer—suffer more than before. Had it just been me, I might have asked you for your protection. But now...I cannot let my mate be hurt. It isn't...no one should suffer what she would if Marta found out what she is to me. I'm sorry, sire, it isn't right that I should talk ill of another of your kind, but I cannot lie to you."

Aaron wasn't surprised by what Tucker told him, but he was about the others hearing about him. Then he realized what Tucker had said. "What do you mean of my kind, Tucker? We, you and I, are of the same species. You said that she is cruel and dangerous. Do you think I'm the same, the same type of master?"

"No, no I don't. But I have...my mate will need me to be able to keep her safe. And we both know that as a human, Sam would suffer greatly in a fight with an older vampire. She will need your protection, too, should I stay within this realm. Asking for protection for me was one thing, sire, but for the two of us…I fear the price would be more than I have."

Price. There was the word again. That did surprise him, on more levels than he wanted to admit. Though he wasn't sure why yet. Did others, other masters, charge their subjects to protect their own people?

"You thought you needed to buy my protection? You think that's the way it works? With what? Help me to understand."

Aaron was mad, not at Tucker, but at the thought of so many like this man going without their mate, their needs, because they didn't have the money to do so. Not just the fear of having a mate and not being able to protect them, but the severe punishment for both of them. If a vampire came to him seeking protection for him and his mate, he would simply give it.

Aaron did take money from his subjects; he wouldn't be able to give them any help if he didn't. But he took it in the form of percentages earned. Vampires had little use for money, and they could live for centuries. Most of them, Aaron included, invested their money in houses, business, and even blood banks. And that money was used to provide for families that cared for vampires during the day, the ones who had no income. The money was used for legal fees if needed, anything and everything they needed beyond the scope of everyday life.

"I have nearly three million dollars saved, sire. It is all yours if you would agree to protect Sam. She is an innocent in this. I never meant to find her, or to bring her any trouble. But if my maker finds her, or even finds out about her…" Tucker shuddered visibly. "She will kill her. I can't let that happen. I will take my punishment and leave. I'll leave the monies with you for Sam's protection."

Aaron sat back and regarded the man before him. He was going to help him and his mate both. He had to. It was no longer a matter of Tucker being a vampire, but Aaron had come to like the couple and wanted them to be able to hang around.

"I need for you to tell me everything. And I mean everything. I want to know your maker inside and out, and all the dirt you have on this bitch, what she did to you and I'm sure others. You need only to pledge your fidelity to me. I don't charge my people for this. In this realm, we work together, help each other. Your money is just that, yours. I will take a percentage of your income from now on, but the other you came with you need to use to keep you and Sam. Can you do that, Tucker? Have you the right to pledge to me?"

"Sire, Sam will..."

"You let me worry about Sam. And Tucker, my man, if I've learned one thing about mates, it's that they can be pretty fierce when they feel cornered. I think once you and Sam bond and mate, you'll find her to be quite the help if you need her. She doesn't strike me as the type of woman who would sit by and want you to take care of her."

"No, sire, she does not." Tucker grinned and so did Aaron. "She seems to be very able and willing to take any measures to make you understand her point of view as well. I do believe if she were a vampire, my maker wouldn't stand a chance against her. Sam would make a very fine warrior."

"I believe you might be right about that. Sara and her have...the two of them could and probably would kick both our asses if they thought we needed it, but I would appreciate it if you kept that little tidbit to yourself." Tucker nodded and the men formed a bond. New and very tender, but a bond of friendship blossomed.

Just before sunrise the next morning, Tucker and Aaron left the study. They had a better understanding of one another—at least Aaron thought so. Tucker told Aaron he felt as if a burden had been somewhat lifted from his shoulders and Aaron felt sick. Sick at the treatment that one of his kind—no, he refused to think of her, this Marta, as one of his kind—could be so cruel to one of her children.

Aaron went in search Sara after showing Tucker where he could rest for the day. Tuck said that he would like to be able to take Sam down with him, and Aaron agreed that would be a good idea. He did tell Tucker that the sublevels couldn't be breached by anyone but the people Aaron or Sara allowed down there. He told them they would be safe in his home.

Sara was in the kitchen, of course, getting the children ready for preschool. He loved this time of the morning when he got to watch them all interact with each other. And after his night, he needed it more than he ever had before.

He noticed that Pete, Dominic's mate and another friend of the family, was there fussing with Lizzy's hair. Finally, Duncan took the stretchy thing from her and showed her again how to pin up a little girl's hair with it.

Aaron knew for a fact that she had been showed several times how to do it and thought she was egging Duncan on again. Aaron laughed at his man; these two had the strangest relationship and no one knew why. He then remembered to talk to her about some of the slang she was teaching Duncan and Mac. Some of it couldn't be rated anything less than X.

"Good morning, everyone. Where are you all off to?" He knew, of course, but it was a matter of tradition that he asked.

"School, Daddy. Just like yesterday and the day before." Mac could sound so grown up at times it scared him.

"Lizzy, has your mother talked with you about...you know?"

He was still amazed at the power she had used to try and get into Sam's head. He was also amazed that Sam had been able to withstand it for so long. When Sam had hit Sara with the blast, Aaron had felt it as hard as Sara had, their bond making her pains his. He was ashamed to remember he had hurt Sam without all the facts.

"Yes, Daddy, and I'm gonna make Sam a pretty picture in school today to tell her I'm sorry. And Tucker, is he gonna stay with us too?"

He kissed her forehead. "I'm working on that, pumpkin." He looked over at Pete and Sara. "I need your help today, both of you. If you can spare the time today, Pete, I also have another project I may need you to look into as well. It's something right up your alley. Game?"

"Sure, I just have to go to Becca's Place to update some security stuff. But I can do that later. Then I have a couple of part-timers down at the electronics store to be trained on some low tech stuff. Whatcha need?" Pete asked.

Becca's Place was a place for abused and battered children to go for safety. It was not species specific, rather just for children. Since it had opened nearly five years ago, the house had saved over a thousand children from abuse, making sure they were well fed, well loved, and eventually finding safe havens for them. Shade and Colin, his best friend, has set it up. And Pete, the resident techie, had made sure the security was the best they could offer them.

"I need you to see what you can find on a Marta Lipscomb, a vamp. She's a master in another realm in Missouri. Also, on Tucker James, he is one of hers." He looked down at his notes before continuing. "I need for you to be very discreet with this. It could mean the lives of Tucker and Sam if she finds out where he is. Tucker said that she is calling him, but she hasn't gotten any closer than when he left. Also, he has an open account at the bank. Make sure it's untouchable by anyone but him for the moment. I don't want Marta to get her hands on what's his. Pete, I can't tell you enough how important it is that she not get a scent about this. She's one nasty bitch."

"Sure. What sort of intel do you need — money, records…just everything? Sara was telling me that she felt Tuck's pain, from this Marta?" At his nod, she continued. "I'll get right on it. The Pack has just put in this new system that I want to play with." She was grinning. It was a grin that he had come to recognize as "I'm so going to enjoy this."

"Everything. Whatever you can find, even rumors, too, if you find some. At this point, assume everything you read, see, or hear is true. This woman is beyond cruel and I won't have you endangering yourself too. It's bad enough that…the things she did, probably still does, is staggering."

"I'll be careful. Tell Tuck that I'll need to talk to him later about some stuff too. Just the usual background, make sure I have the right bitch and all. Sam too." Pete smiled. "Wow, have you tasted any of her stuff? Damn, that girl can bake! And what she can do with chocolate…well, it makes you wanna weep and sing odes to her."

The ribbon in Lizzy's hair was finally finished and Pete left to go have her fun. Aaron was just sitting back to watch his mate eat her breakfast when Mac looked at over at him.

"Daddy, can I talk to you, please, man to man?" Mac had grabbed his father's hand and was holding it very tightly. Something had upset the little boy and Aaron was very worried. Aaron leaned down to scoop the little guy up into his arms and leaned his forehead onto Mac's.

"Sure, but after the night I've had, do you think maybe you could spare a hug or two? It would certainly make things go a little easier for me for the rest of the day. Just having one of those can make everything perfect again."

Aaron knew that Mac needed the hug just as much as he did, but also knew that Mac wouldn't bristle so much when he thought his dad needed them more. It was something the two of them had worked out. Lizzy would hug anyone and everyone, but Mac was a little more cautious. Since preschool had started, Mac had begun to think of hugs as "mushy girl stuff." Aaron knew in a few years Mac would change his mind pretty quick about that. Aaron grinned. He couldn't wait until Mac discovered that "mushy girl stuff" was not as bad as he had thought.

As they made their way to Aaron's study, he thought about how grown up Mac was becoming. Some days he would be his little boy, on others, like today, Mac presented a growing young man.

"I seed...saw Tucker...he was...I..." Mac looked up at his dad.

The little boy blushed and his stammering gave Aaron a little hint as to what he had witnessed. He hoped he knew. The boy was sharp enough to know some things in his home were different than his friends' homes, but he didn't know everything.

"Tell me Mac. What did you see Tucker do to Sam? It's all right. No one is going to be mad at you."

Aaron's heart was pounding. He knew that he and Sara could get a little carried away when they were together, but had never let it get out of hand when the children were about. Tucker didn't have children and neither did Sam. He just hoped that whatever Mac had witnessed, it was not as bad as he was thinking it was.

"TuckerwasgonnakissSamandIdidn'twanthimto.   So   I slammed the door. I don't like him kissing her. She's nice and always smells like chocolate chip cookies. So I hit the door hard instead of knocking like you told me to."

It took him a few seconds to figure out the first sentence. After unscrambling the run along statement, Aaron sat down hard in his desk chair. Whatever he had expected, this was not even close. His son was five years old and jealous because a woman nearly five times his age. Aaron had never had a prouder moment. He sobered up quickly; Sara would be so pissed if she knew that was his first thought.

"Well, hum...Mac, I suggest you talk with Tucker. See what his intentions are toward Sam. You know what mates are, right?" Mac nodded, relief evident on his face. "Well, Tucker has decided that things are too complicated for him to take Sam as his mate. No, that's not fair; things are too dangerous for him to take Sam as a mate. He may be right. He has some horrible people in his life that could hurt her and him as well, so he is planning on leaving her here when he...well, when he...if we can't work things out, Tucker is going to leave us."

How did he tell a kid that a grown man like Tucker James felt he would rather meet the sun than to go back to the hell he had found himself in? How did he explain that as a mated vampire, he could do no less than protect his mate? No matter what it cost him? Not that Aaron blamed Tucker. The fact that he had survived all these centuries as he had said a lot for the man. But now that he had tasted freedom, no matter how small, he wouldn't—no, he couldn't go back to that again.

"Does he like her, Dad? Sam, I mean. Does Tucker like her? He seemed...he acts so sad all the time. Maybe he doesn't love her like you do Mom." There was such hope in his voice that Aaron had to fight a smile.

"Yes, I believe he loves her very much."

"Oh," Mac said as he shuffled his feet. "Okay then. I guess that's okay with me. I'll talk to him later. Okay, Dad?"

"Sure, son. That would be great. I'm sure that Tucker will appreciate it too." Oh, his son's first crush and he had no hope of it ever amounting to anything. Poor kid.

Mac left shortly after that. Aaron sat there for a long time, thinking about the other vamp and the things Tucker had shared with him. Aaron was not sure he could have survived under those circumstances. He had led a reasonably easy life in comparison to Tucker's. Aaron was older by nearly twice Tucker's age. He had lived less but had seen more than Aaron felt he ever would. Sara startled him from staring out into space a few minutes later when she came into the office.

They had an agreement about the office. Neither was to invade the other's thoughts while inside this room when the door was closed. It gave them both a much needed break from the everyday issues and also gave them a break from each other. Sometimes one or both would just come into the big, cavernous room to sit and think about their mate, the words that had been said in anger or in love, the way the children had hurt them in a small way, or the way that they had made them laugh or smile. Secrets were fine between couples and needed, Aaron thought, so long as they were not the kind to fester and boil over into hate and meanness.

Sara didn't pry nor look to see what Aaron's thoughts were about. He knew because he could have felt her if she had. She simply walked over to him and cuddled up on his lap. She held him close to her, letting him get comfort, as much as he needed for as long as it took. Neither said a word, but simply held on.

Pete came in with a short knock and she and Sara began working at tracking down information. When she had left earlier, Pete had said she needed to get another set of eyes and for some reason, he had thought she meant another person. He should have known better. Pete was the greatest computer whiz he knew. When she walked in with two more lap top computers, he burst out laughing.

"Ah, Piccadilly, why is it that you continue to surprise me at every turn?" he asked her, still laughing.

Her fierce glare made him laugh again. "Keep calling me that, fang-boy, and somebody will have to be doing a search for your body parts very soon."

Aaron needed to rest for the day soon, and knew now that he had someone working with him on Tucker's problem, he would rest easier. And the laughter of the morning, along with the hugs, was going to go a long way to helping him too. And having the best would certainly make them quicker as well.

CHAPTER EIGHT

Sam woke up about ten o'clock that morning. She had missed enough work and needed to go in today. The other women who worked for her could help when needed, but Sam didn't have recipes. And she did all the decorating herself. She was not only faster, but much better at it from all the years of practice. Plus, she was reasonably sure that neither woman who worked for her could cook. And if they could, they'd eat everything they did.

Sam rolled to her side. Instead of being alone in the big bed, she was lying next to Tucker. She took a few minutes to look at him. He was handsome with his bold features and hard muscles. Reaching out, she ran her hand up his arm and over his bicep. The muscles there jumped and moved beneath her touch. Then as her fingers continued their journey, she slowly traced the contours of his mouth, first his lower lip, then over the full upper one, pausing slightly when she felt his breath puff slightly from them. Lying back on the bed, she realized that if she didn't leave soon, she wouldn't. He was too much of a distraction as it was. Dressing quickly, she was in the kitchen in a few minutes and in a cab out front in less than thirty. The only person she saw was Penny, the cook.

Her shop was nearly empty of foodstuffs, so Sam began working right away. She always made the things that took the longest to make first, mixing the batter for bread and setting it to rest after ten minutes of hard kneading. Next came the dreaded pie crusts. She hated filled pies of any kind, much preferring baking the crust then filling it. Or her favorites were pudding based or custards, they always looked so pretty when finished. While the crusts were cooling, she began baking the cookies, hundreds of dozens of cookies, chocolate coconut, hazelnut fudge, and orange thumbprints. The iced ones were her favorite, especially when she had the time to draw on them. At any given holiday, she would spend hours just having fun putting all sorts of scenes on the cookies, Christmas being her favorite.

She was just taking the last of the blueberry buckle out of the oven when Sally came back to give her a message. The two women had the shop open when she had arrived and had been taking orders.

"A Mrs. MacManus said she'd like to come by and talk to you tonight ifin you ain't busy. Said she was bringing the kids and a shade of something. We was kinda busy, so I didn't get that too good. Also, wanted to know ifin you got any plain old chocolate chip cookies? Told her we don't make those too much, but I'd ask ya. Got any? Chocolate chip I mean?"

"Yes, I just took ten dozen out for that wedding order. I think there should be about two or so dozen left over. What time did she say she was coming by?"

Sam was hot and didn't want to have to deal with Sara again. She needed to get a lot done before the weekend weddings. And her head hurt. The cut wasn't bleeding, but no amount of pain reliever was cutting through the pounding.

"Well...like I said, we was kinda busy, so she's out there now. Her and some other woman what was here the other day? And a bunch of kiddies." Sally's language was terrible and it got worse by the end of the day. Sam wondered some days how the customers could understand her enough to know what they were getting. Sally laid the message down and started to walk away. Sam glanced up at the clock. It was just after six o'clock, closing time.

"Shit, Sally! A phone message is much more effective if I can get it when it comes in." She stood up to take off her apron and make a quick escape out the door when Lizzy came running into the kitchen.

Sam didn't allow people, especially kids, in her domain. Lizzy stopped about two feet from Sam. Lizzy looked nervous and unsure of herself and of Sam. *Good*, Sam thought. She had hurt Sam and needed to understand that things had consequences.

"Hey kid." Sam was just as unsure about her. She didn't know any other kids but this one and her brother. Sally's children were grown and had moved away, and Betty was living with another woman and they didn't have any plans of becoming parents.

"I came to give you this, and to telled — tell you how sorry I am. I didn't know I was hurting you. I didn't think through my actions."

Lizzy shoved a drawing of a stick person surrounded by cakes of all sizes, some bigger than the person, at her. Sam was touched. She had no doubt that Lizzy had been coached by someone, but Sam was happy all the same.

Sam walked over to her zero doublewide fridge and stuck the picture to the door over several orders that were in mid-fill. Lizzy ran over and hugged her legs, then jumped back at the pop that went through her and Sam. It wasn't always audible, but this time it was.

"Yeah, that's why I don't like to be touched. Didn't hurt you, did it?" Sam reached out and gently rubbed Lizzy's head. Sometimes the energy Sam let off was painful, others just a small static charge.

"No. I didn't know people could pop someone like that. Does that happen all the time?" Lizzy made the last question sound like it had many more syllables than it actually had.

"A lot, yeah. It's because I'm an empath. Do you know what that is?" Lizzy started to nod then changed it to a shake. "Well, I can feel everyone's feelings and emotions, all the time if I don't close myself off to them. The pop is an overload to my system. When you touched me, I get all of you at once and it 'pops' me."

"Does it hurt you?" Lizzy asked her.

Sam was not sure if she should share with a little kid, but figured if she wanted to stay one step ahead of her, Sam would be better served if the kid knew what she was getting into. But when Sam answered her, she looked directly at the two women standing in her kitchen.

"Yes. Well, sometimes, if I'm not prepared for it. I could see you coming full tilt, so I braced myself for it. Usually it's much bigger, but you haven't been around long enough to have that many different emotions pinging through you all the time yet. If you were older, it would have been very strong. Hello, Mrs. MacManus, Mac, how are you guys tonight?"

Sam looked to the door at the back of the shop, wondering if she could make it out the door before Betty and Sally left for the night. Tomorrow she was going to have a long talk with them both about phone messages and the importance of telling them to her seconds before someone showed up.

"Don't even try." Sara looked from Sam to the door, as if to say, "I know what you are planning and I will stop you. I came here to talk to you."

"Well, I have some baking to do, so if you wanna talk, you'll have to do it in here. I've been in and out of injuries of late, in case you hadn't noticed, and I'm a tad behind." Sam went back to her work, determined to ignore them. It was like trying to ignore a thunderstorm in one's own house.

"You've been hurt more than you have been getting at our house? Gosh, you must be really clumsy, 'cause you been hurt a lot!" Mac made it sound like Sam had done nothing but bleed all over the place since she had met him. Which, after careful thought, she probably had.

First she had been shot, which he hadn't witnessed but had seen the aftermath of, then she had been put into a deep sleep to heal first from his mom and then Tucker. Then last night, she was hurt again by being thrown against the wall. Yeah, she thought, she had been really hurt a lot.

When everyone converged in the kitchen, they stared in open-mouthed amazement at everything. There were sugary confections everywhere, different colored icings with flowers and animals standing on them, cupcakes by the yards, and hundreds upon hundreds of cookies cooling on racks. Standing in the corner on a rolling cart was a huge wedding cake with seven tiers and a waterfall made from real silk that Sam told them was a piece of the material used in the bridesmaids' dresses.

"They're supposed to come to get it in the morning. I have to put their names on it here, but first I have to put the finishing touches on it." She pointed to the area just below the bride and groom. "It needs to have a few more of the non-perils put inside the roses to make them shiny. There is also the bridal cake to finish. It's for the two of them to shove in each other's faces."

"How long have you been doing this?" Shade asked as she looked at the table filled with cakes of all sizes. She was delighted by the little six-inch cakes that had been ordered for a little girl and her ten friends to enjoy, each with a different theme of a Disney princess. Sam just thought they were goofy.

"My mom taught me to bake, and to enjoy it. She and I lived in the upstairs of this place until...until later. She was the pastry chef, decorating the cakes and stuff. She would let me play with her tubes of colors. Once I got pretty good at them, she'd let me make the roses first, then I moved up to other flowers and stems."

Sam put the kids, Mac, Lizzy, and Shade's three kids Shamus, Brent, and Caitlynne, on a stool each and handed them a tube of hard icing. The icing really was not hard, but it got hard enough to withstand being stuck on a cake after a few minutes and transported home. Giving them each a sheet of wax paper, Sam gave them the basics of making a flower, starting with a simple daisy and then a quick rosette.

Sara and Shade wanted some of the goodies in the worst way. Sam could practically see the drool on their chins. Shade had her eye on the Philly cheese Danish that had been smothered in cherries jubilee. It was a feather pastry made from layer upon layer of thin dough then after it rested, filled with cream cheese and confectioners' sugar and vanilla. When it was finished baking, Sam had drizzled warm caramel over the top and sprinkled with chopped walnuts. If the customer wanted it to go, the cherries served in a little container on the side were added just before eating.

Sara was eyeing the Mad Mother Maker. It was a large brownie that had been baked in a large cupcake tin. When cooled, hollowed out and filled with thick dark chocolate fudge and candied cherries, there was a dollop of dark chocolate melted and shaped into a heart that sat dead center, and as if that was not enough, rich dark chocolate candy had been melted and streamed all over the top and dripped down the sides to form a puddle of a hard shell under it.

"You know if you want it, all you have to do is ask. I don't make them for show." Sam simply reached into the show trays that had been filled to pop under the glass counter in the morning and handed each of them the treat.

Shade didn't even hesitate when Sam told her that she could have more of the cherries to pour over hers. She just opened the fridge door Sam had pointed to and scooped up another scoop of the beautiful fruit.

When each of the kids had finished and cleaned up their mess, Sam took the best attempt of the roses they had been trying to make and stuck them to the wedding cake. When Sara started to protest about the bride finding those little flowers that looked nothing like Sam's, she pointed out that the bride would do good to notice anything about the cake, much less five little flowers among several hundred others.

They never got to talk about what they had come there to discuss, but that was all right, Sam supposed. They had made up and become friends of a sort. The kids were very happy with their results, and Sam taking their picture with the wedding cake and their flowers went a long way to smoothing out any ruffled feathers the women may have had toward her, at least Sam hoped so. And she was right; no one could tell one flower from the others — at least from a distance.

"Are you going home now, Miss Sam?"

Brent was a very lovely little boy that Sam had taken an immediate liking to. So when he had asked very nicely if Sam would please be able to bake him a "just 'cause" cake, without flowers of course, sometime, she didn't ask if it was all right, simply told him sure.

Sam had explained to them that sometimes people didn't want their cakes to say anything on them; they just wanted a cake just because they could have it, no special reason.

"Later, but I don't have far to go. I'll just go upstairs when I start to fall asleep in the icing. I have a lot more baking to do tonight. I have a..." Sam looked at the women before she continued. "I have something to do tomorrow night."

Sam had another rescue tomorrow night and she was very nervous about it. This move involved a woman and her six kids whose husband had become progressively more abusive as the years went by. The woman had tried to get away on her own a couple of times, but Sam had been told he always found them. The family had to wait until now to be moved. Moving six kids and one adult had proven to be a little more than the system was ready to handle then, that is why it had taken an extra week to get them out.

Last week, he had hit their oldest daughter and had broken her arm in two places. The little girl, Rosa, had missed the bus, which had had a different driver and she had gone the wrong direction, leaving several children to find an alternate way to school that day.

"Need any help with your late night jobs, Sam? I'm sure that I could persuade a couple of men to come along with you."

Sam just glared at Sara's suggestion. She figured that the alpha had told Aaron and he, in turn, had told Sara. Sam didn't care for the way these people kept interfering with her life. And she especially didn't care for the way they thought that she needed help either. She'd been doing fine on her own for some time now.

"Nope. If you think you know something, then spill it. Otherwise, what I do is my business, Mrs. MacManus, and I'd appreciate it if you and yours would mind your own where I'm concerned." Sam leaned against the work table. "I don't mean anything to you and your family and I'd just as soon keep it that way."

"You're going to get yourself killed, is what you're going to do," Sara snapped. "And I don't want you to. I've grown quite fond of those little brownies."

"Like I said, Mrs. MacManus, mind your own business and leave me to mine."

After another twenty minutes of badgering her for information about the job to no avail, the women left, taking several loaves of the fresh bread and a few of the cookies with them. Then Sam went back to the kitchen to finish up the last of the pretty cakes for the display case and to clean up after herself. She didn't leave a dirty kitchen.

She felt him, the man, before she knew what she was feeling. A tingle around her neck and a feeling that whatever it was, it was close to her. She jerked around in her chair to see what was giving her the willies. Tucker.

"I know for a fact that I locked that door when the others left. So, if you don't mind, on your way out again, make sure it's turned to the locked position again. It's sort of tricky, I know, but when I lock the door, that means I don't want anyone to come in. Bye." She turned back to the table she was scrubbing down.

"You have my blood, and it calls to me. I want to talk to you."

That made her jerk back around and look at him. He was closer than she thought. And she didn't like the feeling of being caged in.

"Tough. I'm all talked out tonight. Mrs. MacManus and...oh, wait! She called you, didn't she? Nosey busy body. Why she can't mind her own...look, Mr. James, I have a lot of things to catch up on, so why don't you do whatever you did to walk through my doors and go out again?" She turned back to the table, hoping he'd take the hint.

"No." This time when he spoke, she could feel his hot breath on her neck. She nearly moaned at the heat his closeness seared into her back and onto her skin.

"This isn't...it's important that you...please stop. You need to back away...oh yes, that feels very good."

He was kissing her neck, deep, open-mouthed kisses that she felt to her toes and back again, settling in her core between her legs. "Please, I'm...I don't want you to do that anymore."

~~~

Tucker turned her around and sat her on the stool she was standing next to. He stepped between her legs and started kissing her jawline and just below her ear. She tasted as good as she smelled, warm and his.

"Yes you do. I can feel your need, Sam. It's as deep as mine. Feel me, touch me, Sam."

He took the useless tube of blue icing from her limp hand and cupped her fingers around his hard cock. Her moan of pleasure moved through him, knifing through his body to sharpen his need as well. He kissed her then, his mouth fused to hers as he began leaning her back hard against the table behind her. He devoured her, all of her mouth like it was his last meal and he was going to savor every inch of it, of her.

"Let me in, love; let me taste your mouth." She parted her lips slightly. Taking that as an invitation, he invaded, conquered, and celebrated. His tongue mated with hers, tasting the confections she had tasted only moments before on her tongue.

Tucker needed...everything. He pulled her closer to his body, marveling at the way they fit, her softness to his hardness. He gripped her hips as he pulled her closer and moved between her legs tighter, closer. She was too low on the stool for him to do what he wanted to her, with her, so he cupped her ass in both of his palms, lifted up, and pressed her heat to his erection. He caught her moan in his mouth, felt it as he rolled through her. Sam wrapped her legs around his hips and hooked her ankles behind him while he continued to lift her up and down his shaft, letting her ride him, spiking both their needs.

"Tucker, please...please, I need." She was whimpering, pleading with him. She wanted him was all he could think of.

"What do you need, Sam? Tell me, and I swear I'll give it to you. Just tell me."

She was driving him closer to the edge as she rode him hard, squeezing him tighter with her legs as he pulled her up and down. Never had he wanted like this, never had he needed a woman this much.

"Wall. Take me to the wall. I want to feel you touch me. I want to feel you inside of me. Please, Tucker, please take me."

He turned them both around and took the two steps to the wall. He slammed her against it and pressed harder into her core with is cock. If they kept this up, they were going to have their first climax together fully clothed, he thought, and nearly let it happen. And for as much as he wanted her, he wasn't taking her the first time against the wall.

"Baby, we need to...I can't take you here. I can't be inside of you like this and I need to be inside of you. We have to move upstairs to a bed."

She unhooked her ankles from him, reluctantly, he thought, and moved toward the back doors that lead to what he knew was her apartment. He was behind her, touching and kissing her, pulling her breasts and kneading them, tugging at her nipples from behind. Before they were halfway up the stairs, he had taken her shirt and bra off, throwing them over his shoulder as he went.

The need to touch her bare skin was making him dizzy. She turned toward him and yanked his shirt from his pants, tugging it over his head and throwing it to the floor. When she leaned her mouth in and nipped at his flat, brown nipple, he nearly threw her down on the stair and took her right there.

"Sam, hurry! Christ, we're not going to make it if we don't hurry."

He was right. As soon as she got the lock undone and opened the door, he took them to the floor and stripped off her jeans and panties. He stood up, shucked off his pants and shoes, and stood naked over her. Going commando had its advantages, he thought, as he fisted his cock. He knew that if he dropped back down to her now, he would hurt her, tear her in his haste to make her his.

"Sam, baby, are you a virgin?" He looked down at her in a red haze. "I need you desperately and I don't want to hurt you. I can feel your lack of experience, but I'm not sure if you're a virgin."

"Yes. No." She turned her head. He could feel her embarrassment.

"Baby, you either are or you're not." He thought to ease her out of it. "Have you ever been with a man before?"

He wanted her to say yes, then he could enter her quickly, bury himself in her heat, but he wanted her to say no more than anything he had ever felt. He didn't want her to have been made love to by another. She was his now and forever.

She didn't look at him, but simply reached for her pants. When she started to pull them back on, he took them from her, then picked her up and sat down in an easy chair with her in his naked lap. He could feel her crying, her shoulders trembling slightly as she tried to hide from him. When she pulled from him twice more trying to get up, he wrapped her in his arms tightly and leaned back.

"Tell me. Tell me what I did wrong. Sam, I can't fix this if I don't know what I've done. I won't hurt you, but neither will I let you go when you're hurting like this."

When her cell phone started to ring, he looked up at the clock on the wall. It was two-thirty in the morning. She scrambled off his lap to get it. He was so shocked that he let her go.

"Hello, yes, ¿Hola? Sí, esto es Sam Hunter. Yo…" She was quiet for a very long time, listening to the person speaking on the other end, he presumed. Tucker got up and moved closer to her, not caring if he was being rude or not. "¿Está usted en el hospital ahora?… Sí, estaré allí pronto… Sí. Sí. Saldré ahora. No, no llama a la policía, yo vengo ahora."

As soon as she hung up the phone, she ran to her bedroom. Tucker reached down to get his pants and was pulling them on when she came out, dressed all in black, her hair pulled back and covered in a black skull cap. She glanced at him then down at the floor again.

"I have to go. There's an emergency. You can let yourself out. When you leave, just lock up. I have my keys." She looked at him now. "This can't happen—"

"No."

"Okay, then don't lock up. I'll call Sally and she can come over and lock up." She moved toward the door. He stopped her.

"No, I mean no, you're not leaving here without me." Tucker had a good enough working knowledge of Spanish to know that someone needed her to come to get them. But not good enough to know the why or the who. "You must let me go with you or I cannot allow you go to."

"Allow me to me go? The hell I'm not. I don't answer to you or anyone. Now move." Tucker moved in front of her door, blocking her only way out of the tiny apartment. He just stood there, arms locked over the chest. He knew she couldn't hurt him...well, he hoped not, but he was only reasonably sure she couldn't move him.

"I am going, Sam. And even if you could get around me, which is highly unlikely, I will still follow you." He grinned when she glared. "You are very beautiful when your temper is up."

"Yeah and your timing sucks. Fine, whatever. I'm leaving, you follow." She pulled her gun from her back and put in a clip. With a click of the slide, she had loaded one in the chamber. Then she reached down to her left leg, pulled out the other Glock, and did the same. After holstering the two weapons, she looked up at him. "What?"

"I thought you...never mind." He stepped aside to let her pass.

He stood beside her as she locked up her apartment, and then followed her out to the garage where she had a small car and a very large van. She got into the van and started it up. The engine was so quiet it almost sounded as if it purred. He went to the passenger side and waited for her to unlock his door. When she didn't, he knocked on the window. She hit the auto window and looked at him, confused.

"What now? Am I going too fast for you or something? Make up your mind. I've got somewhere I have to be."

"I can't get in. Will you disengage the lock for me?"

"No, you said you wanted to follow, remember? You said you'd follow and that's all I agreed to. Now move so I can leave."

"Open the door," Tucker growled.

He'd had about enough of her games. He was angry and frustrated. He should have taken her on the table in the kitchen, then they would never had heard the phone ring and he would be still making love to her right now instead of in a garage arguing about a stupid door lock.

CHAPTER NINE

She didn't have time for this crap. So instead of opening the lock, she threw the van into reverse and backed out of the garage, barely missing the toes of the giant who was still screaming at her. She needed to concentrate on what was happening right this moment and he was way too much of a distraction. The man was going to drive her crazy.

Sam pulled in to a parking space about two blocks from the address Maria Schaller, a nurse at the hospital and an underground worker with her, had given her. Sam was set to rescue the family tomorrow night, but it turned into an emergency room situation tonight.

Maria said that the woman, a LaDonna Hermendez had been brought in to the hospital by ambulance about an hour ago badly beaten and bleeding. When she woke up, she started screaming that he, presumably the husband, Juan, would kill the children if left with him. Sam's job was to go and do a pluck and pull as soon as possible. Lives were at stake and more so than usual.

The house was eerily quiet when she walked along the outside walkway to see if anything was going on. There were no lights on in most of the house, but a glow from a front room. Sam had asked Maria not to call the police for one hour, hoping that she was not too late. Sam made her second pass and things were still quiet so she moved up to the back door to get a feel for the house.

Closing her eyes, she reached mentally into the small house and found all the children were alive and the man was in a drunken stupor in the same room with them. It felt like a living room, there was warmth and a hum that usually meant a television was on. She opened her eyes and nearly screamed.

Tucker clamped his hand over her mouth just as she opened it. Had he not, she was sure the entire neighborhood would have heard her. He leaned in to her ear and whispered, "You said to follow you. You should have told me the address and I would have met you here."

She could only glare at him because she didn't trust her voice not to be forty or so octaves louder. Instead, she did something she hadn't done with another person in years. She spoke to him mentally.

"Can you hear me, asshole?" The look on his face might have been worth it if she wasn't so pissed at him.

"Yes, but I am no asshole." He kissed her nose, totally throwing her off. "Why do you persist in calling me names? I have yet to call you anything but Sam. Well, there was just before I was able to ram my cock deep into your wet pussy, I did call you baby. But that was an endearment, not like what you call me."

"Shut up. I don't want to talk about what did or didn't..."

"It definitely didn't happen. I would remember an occasion such as that." He touched her cheek now. He did that a lot—touch her. "But we will finish. I want to feel your heat around me, feel you ride me while I take you. Would you like that, Sam, to ride my cock until we are both spent?"

"Don't do that. I...we aren't going to do that again. You need to get that into that thick head of—"

He took her mouth again, his tongue invading hers and sliding along it like a caress. She wanted him, and felt herself lean toward him and press against him. When he chuckled, she stepped back. She was going to stake him when this was over, she just knew it.

"You must relax. I can feel your terror as though it is my own. I had hoped to distract you for a moment, but I fear all I did was make me need you more."

"I hate you right now." She put out as much anger as she could to make sure he understood she really was. "I don't have time for this. Stay here. I have to go in and get those kids from the drunken sot on the couch."

"I'm not staying here. How do you know he is a drunken sot on the couch? He could simply be a man who is napping with a bottle in his hands." He kept touching her as he talked and it was making her body do weird things. She wasn't sure if she liked it, but she certainly wasn't telling him if she did. He was entirely too sure of himself already.

"Relax, love. You can do it." She knew what he was doing; he was trying to tease her into slowing her heart rate down. She would be dangerous going in strung out like she was. She took a deep breath. It was a mistake. She could smell him. Now her heart rate was up for an entirely different reason. And she hated that he knew that too.

"I can feel him. The children are in there with him." She pulled the gun out and gripped it in both hands. "My job is to save them, yours is to stay out of my way. Got it?" Sam started to move away.

"Wait. I can disable the man from here and we can get the children out. But we do this together, understand?" Tucker whispered through her mind. "There is no reason for anyone to be harmed tonight."

It wouldn't have been so bad, his idea, if he hadn't acted so superior about it.

"I should just shoot you and be done with it. At least in the leg. If I didn't have to carry you to safety if I did, I would, too. And the only reason I'm not is because I don't have time for that. And no, you are not going in there to 'disable' anyone. I am a professional and I'm good at it. So stay here."

"We are going to have to set some ground rules, you and me. I don't like you giving me orders any more than you like to hear them. You will desist this now. It is in my make-up to protect you and that is very difficult to do if you do things that are a danger to you."

She nearly burst out laughing at his arrogance. If she didn't have so many people depending on her right now, she would have shot him. Instead, she decided to give him a piece of her mind.

"Look, fang-boy, you can take your fucking protective DNA and shove then up that tight ass of yours. I will not be your little puppy. I'll bite your fucking ass."

"Now that sounds promising. Do you promise to bite me hard?"

She just stared at him with her mouth wide open and her mind completely blank. Turning on her heel, Sam moved into the house, gently unlocking the door with her mind as she did so.

Sam hadn't lied to Lizzy when she said she was an empath, but she had many other names and abilities as well, telepath, telekinesis, clairsentience and psychometric. She had a very talented mind, too bad she hated it so much.

"We are so going to talk about this," he said to her. She could feel that he was close behind her.

She knew she was revealing a lot of herself, and she knew that she would regret it later. But right now, she needed to do this. They had wasted enough time already. People were waiting for the children to take them to safety.

When they reached the room where they all were, Sam looked at the children. They were huddled in a corner of the little room. The television was blaring out a Spanish sitcom or something. Sam smiled at them and nodded.

"Su madre me envió, yo le necesito para venir conmigo ahora, por favor." She let them know that their mother had sent her, hoping that would calm them down. The smallest of about four was beginning to cry softly. The oldest, the one with a large cast covering her arm, put her good hand over his mouth, much in the same way Tucker had done outside. "Prisa, nosotros debemos darnos prisa. Hurry."

When Juan, the man in the chair, shifted his considerable weight on the couch where he was snoring, the gun in his hand shifted as well. He didn't lose his grip on the Smith & Wesson, but actually pointed it toward his kids. Everyone froze. Tucker walked around Sam without a word and moved to the man. Once Tucker touched Juan's forehead and commanded him to sleep, they all got going again. When Sam had the children out the door and out of harm's way, she watched as Tucker took Juan's gun from him and slipped it into his back pocket.

By the time Tucker came outside, Sam was halfway to the van, carrying one child on her hip and another was hanging around her neck on her back. He flashed himself to her and took the one from her back and picked up another that was lagging behind. Once they were loaded, she gave them each a box filled with a sandwich, bottled water, and some cookies. She was glad now that that part was ready and she'd put them in the fridge in the garage earlier that day. For the baby, she produced a smaller box filled with small, round container of cereal that he could eat and not choke, and a Sippy cup filled with milk. When she seemed satisfied with the arrangement, she got into the driver's seat. But before she could close the door, Tucker was there.

"I'm going with you. You will need to let me in, Sam, please. I sincerely want to help you with this." At her nod, he reached inside the van and opened the automatic locks for the other door. Quickly moving to the other side, he slipped into the van and closed the door. With a quick look back at the children, she took off.

They were silent for about ten minutes when she suddenly needed to pull over. She wasn't surprised by this. She had to do it every time she did one of these removals.

"Stay with them, I have to...stay here." She jerked open the door and ran into the street, narrowly missing an oncoming car. She heard him curse then tell someone to keep everyone in the van until he returned. Sam hoped the kids understood, but kept moving.

He was at her side when she reached the alleyway. She was sick, retching and gagging behind a building just off the street. He walked slowly up behind her and touched her back as she knelt down in the dirt and grime. *No way, did he have to witness this too?* she moaned to herself.

"Don't touch me. Go back to the car," she said between tossing up her dinner. "I want to be alone."

"No, they're fine. Are you all right?"

Stupid question, she was sick. "Yes, I'm just dandy. Go away." He touched her back when she answered him.

"I'm staying here with you, and you are in no position to argue with me."

She didn't answer him. What was the point? Her belly was sicking up the stress of the assignment, just like it always did. She was always worried she would get someone hurt, or worse, killed, and it weighed heavily on her until it was over.

After a couple more minutes of nothing else coming up, she stood and leaned against the building. Then turned and made her way back toward the van. Before she was halfway there, he grabbed her arm and jerked her around to him.

"Why do you do this if it makes you ill? Does your life mean so very little to you?" Anger colored his voice and she could just see his fangs.

"My life means absolutely nothing to me. Nothing! If he had shot me, I would have..." Pulling her arm free of his grip, she went to the van and got in.

She didn't wait for him. She wasn't sure what she would have said to him at any rate. He'd been right to come with her. He'd been right about the man too. But it was the look in his eye when she'd told him her life meant nothing. He'd looked...shocked.

CHAPTER TEN

Tucker stood there long after she left, having gotten in and taken off without waiting to see if he'd continue on with her. The words, the connotation that she would willingly forfeit her life, kept running through his mind. He needed to talk with someone, but he didn't know anyone, didn't have anyone he could call friend. He reached out to the only person he knew and asked to speak to him.

~~~

"She went into a stranger's house and kidnapped the children from an armed drunk tonight. How do I protect her if she does that during the day, sire?"

Tucker was seated in the study again; this time, Sara was with Aaron. Aaron had thought that Sara could shed some light on the girl's behavior as she herself had been a warrior and savior at one time. Sara hoped so.

"I believe she is doing it during the day, Tucker. I've had her investigated. The information I have of her is in and out of hospitals and long nights in jail. She has led a much checkered life if one were to only look at the information given here." Aaron handed the file to Tucker and leaned against his desk. "I've tried everything I know to get information about her, and believe me, if my computer whiz can't find it, it's not findable."

"Who is she?" Sara asked them. "What is she? Because I can't believe either of you believe she's strictly human. I mean, the girl drives me nuts most of the time, but she is wonderful with kids, and Mac is in love with her." She glanced at Tucker and saw the man stiffen. Vampires were a very jealous lot, and she found it amusing that he would be upset about a five-year-old little boy.

"We need to find out. She's Tucker's mate, and as a part of my Kiss, then it is imperative that we make sure she isn't something that could harm us. I don't really think that she is, but she is hiding something."

"Sire, I still haven't...she isn't my true mate. I don't know if she ever will be. You know the reasons and as I have said, they are too great to burden her with at the present. Marta it getting closer, and the moment I take Sam, she will know."

"You let me worry about Marta. I seem to say that to you a lot, don't I? But I mean well. The moment she enters my territory, I'll know. I'm a much older and wiser master than her and have loyalties that she could only dream of. I have decided that you are already a member of this Kiss, Tucker; my family protects what is theirs. You have nothing to worry about, I will see to it." Aaron put his hand on Tucker's shoulder. And we will keep Miss Hunter safe, no matter how hard she tries to say otherwise. But I will tell you this, and I'm making this a demand, Tucker, you must mate with her, mark her. I cannot protect her as well until then. Do you understand? I hate making demands." He glared at Sara when she snorted at that. "I want it done in one week or face the consequences."

"Yes, master."

Tuck left soon afterwards, having given Aaron as much information as he could on Sam's schedule, where she had gone tonight, names, anything and everything they could think of.

"You can't really demand that he mates with her, can you?" Sara had been slightly taken aback by his demands to Tucker; she didn't realize that a master held such power over another vamp.

"No, I can't really. But I'm hoping that by the time he figures that out, it will be too late for either of them. I believe she will be good for him; her ability to be so outspoken and demanding could be just what he needs to be brought out of his shell. He has been browbeaten for so long; it will take a very strong woman to pull him out. The woman Marta is his maker; that's a very hard call to resist, especially in light of the way he was treated by her. No, getting them bonded and mated will serve them both, her safety and his sanity."

Sara thought that if Sam set her mind to anything, she'd succeed. Just thinking about Sam taking her on that day she'd been shot made Sara smile. The girl had guts, that was for sure.

~~~

The next morning, Pete showed up at Sam's bakery. She couldn't believe the incredible smells coming from the place even before she opened the door. The smells of cinnamon and sugar were the most prevalent with fresh baked bread and yeast coming in next. She took a deep breath before she approached the counter.

Pete was mate to Dominic Marshall, and the best computer expert there was. She could also run the tightest security system and had been known to step on the incorrect side of the law just to show larger companies what they were lacking in that department. She was now employed by the Brotherhood of Gray, the largest werewolf pack in the nation, as their security expert. It paid very well and helped donate great amounts of money and time to Becca's Place, a place that held a very dear place in Pete's heart.

"Hi there, cutie, what can I getcha?" Betty didn't say a word to Pete about her face and arms. Most people turned away from the elaborate designs on her face. If people could see her in her natural form, they'd be one of two things; fascinated by the extent of the markings or terrified when the marks moved independently of the woman who wore them.

It wasn't a tattoo, but a crest, a sigil that marked her magic abilities. Pic was a wood nymph, and a very strong one at that. And because of her magic, when Dominic claimed her as his mate and changed her to a vampire too, she didn't lose her ability to be out of doors. Which was great for her, because like all plants of the forest, the one growing on her body needed sunlight and moonlight to rejuvenate and to grow.

"Is Miss Hunter in? I'd like to speak to her please. That is, if she isn't too busy. I was sent here by a mutual friend."

"Oh, Sam's not in right now. She's…hummm…well, she's just not in, but I can take a message and have her get back with you."

Pete could read minds and she had no problems reading this woman's. Sara and Aaron both had warned Pete that Sam was going to be more than a little uncooperative about this. Pete didn't mind; she was used to dealing with stubborn people. She also knew that she was one too. Betty didn't know where Sam was, only that there was stock piled up in the back to go out and a note that said she'd be back before the wedding cake was to be picked up, nothing more. Also, the worry about Sam and the assignments she took on.

Pete was surprised to know that Sam's people knew what she did. Then she realized that Betty was one of her assignments from long ago. But it hadn't turned out quite as easy as the night before. Sam had been injured that night and Betty nearly killed by the woman's live-in boyfriend. He had taken a ball bat to Betty before Sam arrived and had hit Sam once in the head before she was able to take him down with a gun. Betty had been her friend since. Pete was startled by the memories and Pete's respect for Sam jumped a few notches. Pete decided to do an Internet search on what had happened that night to see why neither woman had apparently severed much, if any, jail time.

"If you expect her back anytime soon, I'd like to wait. What I have to see her about is very important." Pete gave her a tiny push to allow her to wait in the back kitchen.

When she was led back there by a bemused Betty, she sat at the desk and looked around. There was nothing there to say anything about the owner of the shop. There was no computer, no phone, no pictures, nothing at all. Pete wandered over to the side by side refrigerator and looked at the drawing that Lizzy had done for her. Sam had gotten a magnet frame and fit it over the childish picture of a room of cakes to protect it. There was also a large daily calendar that had orders, pickup times, and bake schedule written on it in wipe off pen. Pete had to admit, Sam was organized.

"Find everything you're looking for, or would you like to search the upstairs too?"

Pete had felt the moment someone had entered the kitchen with her, but didn't turn around until the woman spoke. When she turned to face the angry woman, Pete was surprised at the beauty standing there staring at her.

"Unless there's a computer or other storage devices, I'm afraid I wouldn't know how to get into it. I'm Pete Marshall, you must be Sam." Pete didn't reach her hand out to shake. She had been warned that she wouldn't take it, and that Sam didn't like to be touched.

"What are you looking for? And no, I don't own a computer. I tend to fizz out things like televisions, computers and such. I once owned a stereo system that every time I touched it, the stupid thing would freak out." Sam walked over to the calendar and made a notation Pete didn't understand. "State your business and get out. You smell like alpha, and I don't care for him at the moment."

"I see, well, I'm not here for Bradley, but I do work for him. I'm the pack's and Aaron's security expert. That's why I'm here. Tucker wanted me to install a security system for you, in both the shop and the apartment upstairs. You can call them if you need a reference."

"No need for them. I trust you're not lying."

Pete started to relax. Maybe this wasn't going to be as hard after all. But Sam's next statement dashed that thought.

"Sorry you wasted your time, but no. Now, if you don't mind, I have things to do."

Sam walked into the walk-in freezer and pulled out the supplies she would need to bake. Ignoring her, she got out a box of eggs from the walk-in refrigerator and started breaking them in the large mixer. Pete didn't mind. She was just as stubborn as the next person.

"I don't offend easily, so I can wait you out." With that said, Pete moved the desk chair over to the farthest wall and sat down. It was just after eight in the morning, she noted, and sat down to fill in the time with work or until Sam threw her out. She hoped it wouldn't come to that, but who knew.

The bride and her mother showed up an hour later, thrilled beyond words with the cake. The delivery men who had come with them carefully loaded the cake and the top into their special truck and left. When Sam closed the back door after declining an invitation to the wedding yet again, she went back to work, still not speaking to her. Pete grinned, just knowing that she would win this battle of wills.

At two-thirty, Pete was getting mad; by four she was downright pissed. When Sam walked to the front of the shop to lock up at six, Pete was ready to concede defeat. Not once in ten hours did Sam even look in her direction. Pete had even tried talking to her. When that didn't work, she pulled out her cell and began making calls and checking emails. The day had not been a total loss. Pete had figured out the lack of computers and other electrical equipment. Even the cash register was an antique kind that required no power. Pete had noticed that when the other women had gone to lunch and Sam had watched the front while they'd been out.

Every time Sam got close, Pete noticed that she either lost the connection or her phone would glitch out altogether. When Sam returned to the kitchen to begin yet another round of baking, Pete tried again to speak to her.

"Sam, I know how the men are of Aaron's Kiss, arrogant, overbearing and damned near stupid with their old fashioned ways. But I've also noticed that they are loyal, loving, and would die for any of us. Tucker seems like an okay guy, and I believe Aaron is right when he told him he had to bond with you by the end of the week. When you mate with him—" Pete stopped and backed up several paces when Sam stiffened and energy poured into the room. "Shit, you're strong."

"What did you say? Mate? As in sex? Are you saying that Aaron demanded that Tucker fuck me by the end of the week? Or what, he'll do it himself? He'll cut off Tucker's dick? What? I'd really like to know, and don't even try lying to me, because if I have to, I will get the answers myself. And believe me when I say, you will not like my way."

Pete was pretty sure she wouldn't either. "No, nothing like that. It's just that you and he are mates. He's…Tucker is your other half, the one that will complete you. And as for Aaron doing it himself, I'm going to pretend you didn't say that. That's just not right; he loves Sara and she, him."

"Are you fucking kidding me? Aaron loves her, yet can demand...demand that Tucker and I have sex?" The room tightened again. Pete was getting nervous. "That's just great. So, was there a particular way he wanted us to do it, do you know? Maybe he'd like to be there to make sure it's done right."

"That's enough, Sam." Tucker's voice vibrated through the kitchen, strength and authority resounding from him. Pete had never been so happy to see someone in her entire life.

Pete moved toward the door, hoping no one would notice that she was making a hasty retreat. She needed to contact Aaron and tell him what she had done. She hadn't meant what she said to Sam. She just wanted the other woman to be happy and know that she was going to be safe and loved from now on. She guessed she might have used a bit more tact, but she was bored and hadn't spoken to anyone all day. No excuse, she knew.

Fuck the power that woman had. Pete was sure it wasn't just magic either, but something more, something mental too.

CHAPTER ELEVEN

"You might as well leave with her. I'm not in the mood to be fucked tonight, but thanks anyway." Tucker felt her hurt. And from her, he felt it as his own. He wanted to comfort her, take her into his arms and hold her, but he knew at this time she'd rip a strip of hide off him in a second. He smiled at that.

Instead, he moved up behind her, started to reach out and touch her, but she pushed away from the counter and went to the door. She locked it, and went to the stairs to her apartment. When she got to the top, he stood at the bottom of the stairs and looked up at her when she turned her back to him again and went inside. Once she was inside, he heard the door lock click shut. He was amazed at her control. He could tell that she wanted to slam it shut and hurl something at him. Wondering what she might to do him now, he turned off the kitchen light and slowly followed her up the stairs.

Tucker was standing in the doorway when she came into the bedroom. Completely ignoring him, she stepped into the bathroom and turned on the taps to the bathtub. Even with her back to the door, he saw her stiffen when he walked in. Filling it with her scent, honeysuckle and gardenias, she stripped down and sank into the deep hot water.

She didn't move when he sat on the toilet next to the old fashioned, claw-footed tub. "My mother took the locks off of

123

doors when I was a little girl. I'll have to make sure I put stronger ones on here."

"I can go through the doors and locks. You won't be able to keep me out. I told you before that you have my blood and it calls to me." Tucker wanted...no, he needed to touch her. "Sam, I'd like to talk with you about what Pete said to you. She shouldn't have said anything. I'm not even sure how she found out, but I — "

"I don't care. I'd really like it if you were to leave. I've had a very hard couple of days, and I have two wedding cakes to make tomorrow. People pretending to care about each other all over the place now days."

He was getting frustrated with her, at himself as well. He didn't know what to do with her. "Sam, please, you have to listen to me. There are things you need to be made aware of. Things that could save your life. I need you and you need me."

He wasn't going to leave her, not tonight. If she wouldn't admit that she needed him, then he would show her how much he needed her. He moved closer to the tub and stopped. The pain started in his legs, and then moved up to his hips. It took him a few minutes of discomfort before he realized it was her.

"It will only get worse. In about fifteen minutes, your head will begin to pound and your heart rate will speed up. I will make it increasingly more painful until you leave. And every time you step into this shop, it will begin where it stopped when you left. I want you to leave, right now, Tucker. I don't want to see you again."

As soon as his nose started to bleed, he shimmered from the room. He knew that if he stayed, she would watch him bleed out until he was drained. He materialized in the lair that Aaron had lent him. He had to think and plan. Satisfied that he had things in order, he crawled into bed. When the sun came up the next morning, he had a plan in place. Heaven help the woman who had taken his heart.

~~~

"Miss Hunter, I'm Officer Justin List of the...local police department. I have a warning...warrant for your arrest. Would you come with me please?"

Sam had just walked out of the shop and was headed to her garage when the "Officer" List stepped up beside her. She reached into his mind and was blocked. She pushed harder, not caring if he felt it or not, and made the man stiffen with the slight pain. But she knew the source.

Justin had been warned that she was mentally strong, but that Sara would protect his mind from her. Justin was aware of her touch. As were, he would know the mental touches when someone touched his mind. But he had come into her domain and all bets were off.

"I see. Officer List, you are just a pawn in this little game, so I won't hurt you, but 'hell hath no fury like a woman scorned.'"

"Ma'am?"

She could almost feel sorry for him. Almost. "Never mind." She followed him to his car and stood by the back door when he went to the front.

"Oh no, let's do this up right, shall we? So, are we going to the mansion, pack house, or are you to take me to the station?"

"Hummm, we are...I guess to the mansion. Miss Sara said that you would hurt me if I let you know about the plan. I guess you're not going to, huh?" The man actually looked relieved. She hated to burst his bubble, but she meant what she said about fury.

"No, I'm not in the habit of shooting the messenger." No, she wanted to shoot the man or men who had sent him. "But as we've already established, you aren't really a cop. What do you say we just lay it all out on the table? Who are you really?"

"I'm a werewolf that works for the Brotherhood as a cook. How did you know? I practiced everything they told me. I don't think I missed anything."

"You did well, but...you did mess up what you had for me, but that's no biggie. What you didn't do was check for a weapon." She put the Glock to his temple and calmly explained what the revised plan was. "This is a loaded Glock forty, Mr. List, and there is one in the chamber, and hot. As in ready to kill if I pull the trigger. What you're going to do is contact your alpha through your mind link and tell him that I have you hostage. I can understand you and will be able to hear you, so go ahead."

He nodded and left his hands on the steering wheel. Smart guy her Mr. Justin. It really was a shame his boss wasn't.

"Alpha? I...it's Justin, my lord."

"How's it going, Justin? Have you picked up Miss Hunter yet?" Sam could hear the amusement in his voice. "And I hope that you were extremely careful."

"I messed up once or twice, sir. And about that, she is...Well, sir, I have a gun pointed to my head, well, she has her gun pointed to my head, quite closely as a matter of fact, my lord." Justin smiled at her in the rearview mirror. "She is listening to us, said she can understand. Sir, no one mentioned checking her for a gun, so I didn't." Justin swallowed loudly. "That would have been something to know, my lord.

Bradley didn't answer right away. He was too busy cursing the young woman who had out foxed him again. She could understand that and through her link with Justin, she could hear every thought that ran through his head. Someone should teach the alpha about blocking, she thought.

"Miss Hunter, are you planning to hurt our young Justin?" He was snapping and, for now, she decided to ignore that.

"If you bothered to get to know me at all fuck face, you'd have your answer. What the fuck is this all about now? Don't you have better things to do than harass me?"

"Yes, but I did this for a friend, for your master. Aaron wants to talk to you and since you won't cooperate, he moved on to desperate measures. Had you have talked with him and Tucker, this could have all been avoided."

Sam didn't think now was a good time to piss her off more but then doubted he was any happier. "Ah, so the bloodsucker and his sidekick have decided, have they? Well, we'll see about that. Justin is fine, but I think I will keep him for the day. If anyone furry or dead comes near me or my shop, Justin will cease to exist. Do I make myself perfectly clear?" She wouldn't hurt him, but the alpha didn't need to know that.

"Yes, but let me make something clear to you, Miss Hunter. If you harm one hair on his head, you will suffer like you never imagined." His voice was sharp, even in her mind. "Do I make myself clear?"

"Bring it on, asshole; I have nothing to live for so if you think to threaten me, go for it. You will regret fucking with me." She cut the connection between them as if she had slammed down a phone. She was sure that Bradley felt it as if she'd punched his ear drum.

~~~

Duncan answered the phone in the kitchen when it rang and then passed it to Sara. It took her a good ten minutes of just simply listening to Bradley rant and rave before she could speak and then it was only in half sentences.

"She fucking had a gun to his head. What kind of woman puts a gun to a man's head and makes him call me?" He had asked this same question twice now. "Is she that stupid?"

"You did back her against a wall, Bradley? And as much as it pains me to agree with her, you brought this all on yourself. None of you —" He cut her off.

"You can't possibly think that this is my fault! Damn it, Sara, I was doing what your mate told me to do." She could almost see him pacing. "I sent a man to bring her in so that she would have to let us take care of her."

"And what makes you think that you wouldn't have done the same thing she's doing right now? No, let me change that, you would have ripped the throat —" This time his growl cut her off. She was getting pissed herself now.

"I would have been calm about it! She said that if any of us — furry or dead — shows up, she'd kill Justin. I don't like it when someone threatens one of —"

Sara had enough. "Now you listen here you overgrown pup. You are the one who sent Justin to get her. You're the one who sent out three men to follow her. You're the one who thought that he was so invincible that one little human couldn't harm the great alpha. She has beaten you at every turn. And the more you push, the harder she pushes back. I told you this wouldn't work. I told you to let her figure this out on her own, but no, not one of you listened to me. Now I'm going to have to go there and see if I can rescue poor Justin. If you so much as lift your leg to piss on a dead log on this property until you hear from me, I will neuter you." The phone slammed so hard she cracked it.

Sara felt the tears threaten. Duncan simply nodded, opened the door under the telephone stand, and pulled out a brand new phone still in the box. She watched him replace the broken one and thought about what the men in her life had done.

She had told them this wouldn't work, that playing this childish game on someone whose mind was as strong as Sam's was going to backfire. And it had. Big time.

Sara was concerned, however, about Sam thinking she had nothing to live for. She had heard this twice now about Sam. Sara thought it might explain why she'd taken such chances with helping the children the other night, and with the story that Pete had gleaned from Betty yesterday. It seemed that Sam may be trying to get herself killed. Sara was sure there would be more to the story about the man in the bakery the first time she had met Sam. She intended to find out.

Sara was also concerned about Sam's plans for Aaron and Tucker. She wasn't worried about either being killed, Aaron was now an immortal thanks to her blood running through his veins, and Tucker was Sam's mate. She wouldn't be able to harm him either. But just in case, she put a little magic around both men just to be sure. She asked Duncan to pick the children up from pre-school and drove into town. First stop, the bakery.

"Hi, I'd like to speak to Sam, is she in the kitchen?" Sara didn't wait for an answer; she just plowed right through to the back when she got to the bakery.

"Come on in, Mrs. MacManus, won't you join us?" Sam and a large man were sitting at her big work table making flowers.

Well, she was making flowers, Sara realized, hundreds of them by the looks of it. Justin was squirting blobs onto the wax paper squares and then eating his mistakes. Neither seemed to be terribly concerned about the others jobs.

"You don't look any worse for wear, Justin," Sara said to the man.

Actually, she was relieved that he was all right. For as much as she told Bradley that Sam wouldn't harm Justin, she had been a little worried.

"No, missus. Miss Sam and I have been getting acquainted, and she's showed me how to bake up a mean apple pie." Justin stood and stretched. "Miss Sam, would it be all right if I took a little stretch? The missus looks ready to explode to talk to you."

And Sara was, too; she was a woman on a mission.

"Sure, Justin, thanks for your help. I don't suppose you wouldn't mind going down to the deli and picking up the lunch I ordered for us all? Tell Betty to give you some cash from the drawer. And take your time; Mrs. MacManus thinks she has a lot to explain to me."

He left; the two women in the kitchen could hear him talking and flirting with Betty and Sally. When the little bell over the door chimed him leaving, Sam looked up from her flower and grinned. "You thought I'd kill him. That's good. No point in making a threat if no one believes you'll carry through with it. I'm kind of busy right now, Mrs. MacManus, so I'd appreciate it if you stated your business and got out of mine."

There were hundreds of tiny little pink roses in front of Sam, all of them the same size and perfectly matched. They were lined up in perfect lines on a large display tray. Sara didn't want to be impressed, but damn it, she was. Sara continued watching Sam, forgetting for a moment why she was here.

"Well?" The hostility was thick in Sam's voice. "I've had about enough of you people, all of you coming in here anytime of the day or night and thinking that I am some sort of part of you. I'm not. I just want to be left alone. By all of you."

"I'd like to call a truce between you and me. I have some things to say and I'd like to not fight with you until I'm finished. There are things you need to know, things that are very important to Tucker and his life."

"Go ahead, but as you are aware, the stipulation to Justin staying alive was none of you to bother me today. I have four wedding cakes for this weekend and taking time out to kill him now is going to put a dent in my plans." Sam didn't even look up from the rose she was currently forming, but reached her left hand down to her side and unclipped her weapon from her belt. She laid it on the table next to her and picked up her tube of pink icing again.

"You'd like me to think you're some sort of murder, wouldn't you? I don't believe you have it in you to shoot anyone, Sam. I think you're a very hurt woman who needs someone to care for you." Sara felt the first touch of fear when the gun hit the table, but then she realized that for whatever reason, Sara trusted Sam.

"Frankly, I don't give a shit what you think of me." Sara could see her fighting the tension. "I'd like for you to take Justin with you when you leave. You people obliviously don't respect boundaries. And you're right, I was never going to kill him, but you know if that fucking dog were here right now, I might be hard pressed not to neuter him with a rusty knife."

"Funny, that's almost exactly what I told him not an hour ago. All right, I'll take Justin with me, but I still don't believe you'd hurt anyone without cause. Have a good day, Miss Hunter; I'm sure we'll be seeing each other again."

Sara left and took a very reluctant Justin with her. He couldn't say enough good things about the way Miss Sam had treated him, how she had given him a whole bunch of her mother's recipes. And despite being afraid when she'd put the gun to his head, Justin really enjoyed Sam's wit and charm.

Sara burst out laughing at that, wondering what the others thought of Sam's "charm."

~~~

Tucker showed up just after sunset. He was there to talk to her and nothing more. He had made arrangements with Aaron to leave the following night. He didn't want to hurt her anymore.

When he got to the bakery, the woman behind the counter, Sally, said that Sam had just gone upstairs to change, she thought she had a date with that nice young man that delivered the staple goods.

"He's been asking her out for an age, poor young man. Sam finally said yes to him today. He nearly fell all over himself he was so excited." Tucker took to the stairs to her apartment as soon as he heard that Sam had a date. He smiled slightly when he heard Sally say, "He probably forgot his wallet" to the bewildered customer who had come in just after Tucker had.

"Where do you think you're going? You are not going out tonight."

He didn't have any rights to her. He had told Aaron that he was moving away to keep her safe, and here he was yelling at her when she was doing just what he wanted. What was wrong with him, he wondered?

"Come in and sit down for a while, so glad you could visit." Her voice was hard, belying her soft words. "Don't you ever friggin' knock, or come through a door?"

Tucker watched her button her shirt, her fingers moving along the seam and pushing buttons through the hole before moving on to the next one. He found it to be incredibly sexy. He felt his cock harden again. Damn it, he wanted her.

"I asked you a question. Where do you think you're going?"

"Actually, numb nuts, you didn't just ask, you demanded. But I don't know why that should surprise me, that's all you ever do. Now I want you to get out. Mickey is coming by and we are going to do the nasty all night long." When she turned away from him, he snapped.

He was across the room in two heartbeats. One second he was fuming in the doorway to her bedroom, the next he had her pinned between him and the wall. He looked down at her, his eyes turning with his need and anger. She had pushed him too far with her sarcasm, and he had already been near the edge.

"Don't..."

"Too late." He lowered his head and brushed his mouth across hers, gently, softly at first. When her small pink tongue darted out and licked his taste from them, he leaned down and ate at her soft mouth voraciously, gorging on her taste, the heat of her. He pulled her body against his, and then pressed them both into the wall. He cock was hard, aching to be inside of her. His fangs, needy before, now elongated, bursting from his gums, the need to sink them into her overwhelming.

"Sam, I want you. Please, baby, I want to make love to you now. Call your date and tell him...tell him he's not to come here. Not ever again"

"I already have," she told him softly. "Please just go home. I want you to go now."

"I won't. I can't."

He felt her tense, then pull back. He could feel her fear, her uncertainty, and he pulled back as well. When she lowered her head and turned away, Tucker lifted her chin and forced her to look at him.

"Tell me, love. Please. I know you hurt. I'm sorry if I—"

"I can't...I have to...please, there's something I have to tell you. You need to know what I am. What I've done."

He pulled away. He wouldn't force her, couldn't, not the way he had been treated for nearly all of his life. His breathing was harsh, his heart pounding. He backed up one step, but held her, not able to let her go just yet.

"Sam, I know you have no reason to believe me, none at all after the way I've treated you, but I won't hurt you. Whatever you have to tell me, I'll understand. I want to be here for you." He knew at that moment, he really wanted to be. He couldn't leave her, not now, not ever.

"I've murdered five people, I'm a failure, and I've killed five people in cold blood."

CHAPTER TWELVE

Tucker didn't answer, didn't say anything, couldn't. But he did watch her, watched as she stood up and began unbuttoning her flannel shirt. He knew this wasn't about sex. This had moved beyond that.

"My mother was a very beautiful woman. She was alone save me, but we...we had each other. She did her best by me, kept me safe. We lived well until the night I turned fifteen. My entire life changed that night. Nothing was...they took everything from me."

Tucker moved to the bed and sat down. He knew in that instance, that second, that he loved Sam Hunter. He loved her with all of his being. And his heart hurt for her.

"We were out in an open field picking wildflowers by moonlight. We were having fun. It was something she and I did all the time, different fields, different nights. It wasn't until they were there—four men and two women—that we realized we were in danger. They were suddenly just there. They came upon us from nowhere. It was magic, you see. They had just shimmered right in front of us."

The flannel came off and then she began unbuttoning the shirt beneath it. When she was down five of the seven buttons, she opened it to her bare skin. Tucker could see the bullet hole scars very clearly now in the harsh light of the overhead.

"They raped us both, brutally. Each of them, including the women, taking turns with my mom and me. My mother fought them. I couldn't. You see, I was scared out of my mind, paralyzed with fear. I just let them rape me over and over. When they were done, they tied her to the ground, driving stakes through her hands and feet, and then used her clothes to gag her. I just laid there until one of the men, the leader I suppose, pulled out his gun and shot me six times. Then they just left, their laughter still echoing through the air." Tucker wanted to go to her, simply hold her, but knew that she needed to purge this. "Mom tried to heal me. She was a very power mage and even in her weakened state, she was able to stop the wounds from bleeding and save me. I suppose she thought she was doing me a favor. I woke up two days later. I spent seven months in the hospital, physical therapy, surgeries, anything they could think of to keep me alive, no matter how much I begged otherwise."

"Sam, you—" She cut him off without even hearing him, Tucker was sure.

"On my next birthday, I killed the first woman. I found her in a little house in Michigan. She was torturing a little boy. The next one, one of the men, died in his car. I'd torn his throat out and watched him bleed to death. Men two and three were ice fishing out in the middle of Lake Erie when I found them. A quick toss of a stick of dynamite and pow! No more. The two women they had locked up in the ice house to use whenever the urge hit them, I suppose. They were already dead by the time I found them. The last man was a were. I found him here. His death was slow and long. I covered his body in silver dust. Did you know they can't heal when silver is involved? Anyway, I covered his body in cuts.

Not really enough to kill him, but enough to give off a scent. He was eaten alive by the same creatures he ran with. Animals, just like he was." She looked at him now, her eyes full of tears.

"I've failed so many people, people who depend on me, that I am weighted down with the guilt. I don't have it in me anymore to be caring. I'm not sure I ever did." She walked toward the door and opened it. "I'd like for you...please just go, Tucker."

"The man, the one from here, do you know his name?" Tucker had a sudden understanding of fate, how things that went around, always came around.

"Peterson, Robert Peterson. Why?"

"That man killed the little girl Becca, the one Becca's Place is named for. I've heard that Bradley is looking for him, has been for several years. This Peterson prick, he was a member of his pack. Bradley thought he had moved to another area. I'd like to tell him, let him know about this man."

Tucker had heard about Peterson the second day he had come to this area. People, especially other supernaturals loved the story about how the house cared for and loved all those children.

"Yeah, go ahead. The alpha wants me dead anyway. I think that would probably push him over the edge. I know some packs have a law about in-house stuff. Lock the door on your way out. I'm going to bed. I'm very tired."

"All right." He turned after a few seconds and left the bedroom.

He went down the stairs and locked up the kitchen. As he was turning off the lights, he contacted Aaron through their link and told him that he would like to set up a meeting between him and the alpha as soon as possible. And that he was staying with Sam tonight.

"I talked with Pete when she returned from the bakery tonight. She feels badly about what she did to Sam. So do I. Tell her that she has my deepest apologizes and that I will do everything in my power to make it up to her," Aaron whispered to him.

Tucker could hear the sorrow in his voice and Tucker didn't doubt his sincerity.

"I will, sire. Aaron? I have a request. I would…do you think it's possible that Sam and I could stay here? I will talk with her. I know that she'll need to pledge to you as well. We've very little to offer you as subjects — "

"Tucker, it will be an honor to have a man such as yourself in my Kiss. We'll work out the details later. For tonight, bond with your mate. The rest will fix itself, you'll see."

When Tucker got back upstairs, he watched as she took off her t-shirt. He leaned against the door jamb and watched her. When she was just taking off her bra, she looked at him. Her expression said that she was surprised to see him.

"The building is locked up. I also made sure that the ovens were off and that everything was put away." He slowly moved into the room. "Aaron said to tell you that he's sorry about Pete. He'd like to make it up to you."

"I thought you'd gone," she said as she covered her breasts with her shirt. "I don't understand. Why are you still here?"

He decided to ignore her questions and move on with the night. Need to hold her rippled along his skin and he moved more into the room. "I also took the phone off the hook while I was out there. I don't want us to be interrupted tonight." He moved to within a few feet of her, just close enough that he could see her eyes. They had darkened.

He slowly moved toward her, pulling his shirt from his jeans as he kept watching her face. She was still staring at him when he moved to stand just in front of her. She had stopped removing her own clothes. Her bright green bra peaking from the edges made his mouth water and his cock burn with need.

He skimmed his fingers down her arms, the need to touch nearly impossible to resist, so he didn't. Then he did the same to her breasts, running just the tips of his fingers lightly over the top of each breast as they spilled out over the top of her bra, never taking his eyes from hers.

"We're going to make love, you and me. We are going to take it slow and easy, stopping whenever it gets to be too much for you. Understand me, Sam? I'm going to touch you, every inch of your delicious body, inside and out." He leaned his face down to hers, looking her in the eye. "I'm not going to hurt you, baby, never will I hurt you. No one shall ever hurt you again, I swear to you."

He kissed her gently this time. His need was there, but this one was tempered with understanding and love. Because he did, he loved her with all of his being; he didn't know how he'd ever thought to leave her.

Tucker touched her cheek, and slid his hand behind her head, tilting her head and bringing her closer to him. He touched the skin exposed just below her ribs at her waist. Her skin was warm, almost hot, and as smooth as anything he had ever touched before. Moving his hand more, he traced his fingers down her spine and back up again. Her moan of pleasure was captured in his mouth and mingled with his own.

He moved his mouth down her neck to her throat, tasting and nipping at the long column. When his tongue touched the rapidly pounding pulse, he felt her shudder and push closer to his mouth. He nipped at her jugular with his fangs, not breaking the skin but scraping over the blood filled vein, almost hearing the beat of it pulse near the surface of her skin. He needed to drink from her, wanted to mark her as his, taste her.

He reached out gently with his mind, wanting to connect and tell her what he wanted, see if she was all right with him touching her. He felt her mind open for him; he pushed in and showed her with thought what he wanted and all that he was feeling. She hissed out her approval, giving back to him what she needed as well.

He bent, scooped her into his arms, and carried her to the bed. When she was standing up again with the back of her legs at the mattress, he pulled back to finish undressing them both. Her whimpers of need along with her touch nearly tore him apart inside when his warmth left hers. His cock was straining to be inside of her, only her hesitancy keeping him from ripping her clothes from her body.

"I want to see you, all of you. I want you naked, now, Sam. I won't leave you. I'm not even sure I can. But you just say the word, baby, and we'll stop. Don't ever think that you can't tell me no. Not that you have any problems with that anyway. All right?"

For an answer, she reached up and pulled him to her mouth again. He could feel that she was unsure. He continued kissing her, reached up and pulled the shirt from her fingers, and let it drop to the floor beside them. He unclasped the front closure to her bra next, leaving it in place as he kissed her. Pulling back slightly, he looked down at the bounty just behind the green lace. He reverently cupped his hand beneath the bra and touched her, filling his hands before he thumbed the lace out of his way.

Her breath caught and her heart skipped several beats as he moved his thumb across her hard, erect nipples. Those tiny sounds made his own heart echo hers. She watched his face, looking for any sign of revulsion, he was sure. But he only saw her and her flawless skin. There was a scar just to the left of her areola and he kissed it. He looked at her and smiled. "Beautiful," He said, and kissed her again.

Picking her up again, he laid her onto the bed, marveling at her beauty. Tucker took several deep breaths to calm himself, to control his need. He had never wanted so badly in his existence. But he could do this, would do this for her.

"If I touch you, I'll explode. I'm so close to coming it's consuming me. Undo your pants for me, unsnap them, please?" His voice was deep with hunger and his arousal. He watched as she did as he asked, her hands trembling slightly and the zipper was giving her problems. When she got the tab finally pulled down, he put his hands at her waist and pulled them off, leaving her matching panties on. He was afraid if she was completely naked he'd lose control and come all over them both before he even began. He smiled at her.

"Magnificent!" Her legs now hung over the edge of the bed. Before she could move back, he knelt down to the floor between her open legs and ran his hands up her feet to her knees and down again.

"I've tasted you before, Sam; I needed to see you and you were naked, the moonlight creasing you skin like now." Tucker kissed her thigh and watched her. "I couldn't stop. I needed to touch you, taste your cream. I came with you, shooting my cum in my hand rather than inside of you. I want to be inside of you this time; I want to come deep, deep inside of you."

Her answering groan had him kissing her knee, her calf, and her shin. Each kiss made her tremble, each made him need more.

"Yes, oh please, Tucker. I need you, please. But I don't...I've never done this before. I've always been so...I'm afraid."

He ran his hands up to her thighs, spreading them further apart for him. When he reached her panties, he slid his hands under both sides and while he watched her face, tore them from her body. Tucker entered her mind and showed her what he was going to do to her, with her. So just as her panties were torn from her body, she came, just as he wanted. Her climax hit her hard, tearing through her, ripping a scream from her throat. Before she came down, while her body was still jerking and contracting, he buried his face in her heat.

Tucker sucked her cream into his mouth with his tongue and lips, flooding his body with her essences, drinking from her. He reached down and ripped the snap from his own pants, nearly tearing the zipper from them as well in his haste to be free. His cock sprang out of its confined space and he grasped it with his fist. He began to stroke it fast and hard while he fucked her as deep as he could with his mouth and tongue. As soon as she came again, he quickly stood and crawled up her body, licking and nipping at her. He lathed her left nipple, pulling it deep in his mouth, and suckled hard. She arched up and pushed her breast into his mouth, begging without words for him to take more. He sucked harder, pulling more of her flesh into him.

"Sam, I want...please, I need to be inside of you. Now, baby, now."

His cock was just at the entrance of her core, the heat and wetness pulling at him, actually pulling him into her. Sam lifted her legs and wrapped them around his hips, canting her hips to take him in. Tucker's control snapped and he slammed deep into her, touching her womb, over and over as he pistoned deep inside of her. He was so close, his balls tightening to his body. He wanted to make it last, to prolong the pleasure for them both, but she was milking him, pulling, and it became too much. He nuzzled her neck, instinct taking over. He wanted to...no, needed to drink from her. Before he could ask her, she tilted her head and pulled his mouth to her.

"Take, take all of me. Please, please bite me, Tucker," she begged him, her voice rough and low.

His fangs elongated more, stretching from his gums. He struck fast and clean, opening her jugular and drawing her hot, spicy blood into his mouth. His first swallow sent him over the edge. He jerked hard into her again and again, emptying himself of his seed, bringing her right along with him. He took one more pull on her vein then after a quick lick to seal the tiny holes, he collapsed on top of her.

As soon as he could move again, he rolled to his side, pulling her lax body with him to drape her across him. He pulled her tight, hugging her to his body and his heart. He started to ask her if she was all right, if he had hurt her in any way, when he heard her soft snore emanating from her mouth. For the first time in more centuries than he could remember, he was smiling as he drifted into a light slumber.

He woke an hour later to a cold, empty bed. She was gone from the tiny apartment. He reached for her and felt that she had gone down to the kitchen just behind the shop. Tucker could feel her emotions were in turmoil, rioting through her, changing with each breath she took. He got up and pulled his jeans on, grinning at the missing snap.

He stood in the doorway from the stairs and watched her work. She seemed to be gluing tiny flowers, roses it looked like, onto a large round cake, more than likely one of the wedding cakes she had mentioned earlier. He didn't realize she knew he was there until she spoke.

"I don't want a relationship with you, well, with anyone really. I...we can't be...what I mean is that...I'd like for you to leave now. You can't come back here."

"It's too late for that, Sam. You're mine. We are a bonded and mated. There is no going back for us." He realized that he was glad for it, for their bond.

"See, that's what I mean. I don't want to belong to you. I...you can...you can go tell your lordy guy that you've done as he asked and that'll be the end of it. He won't have to...to whatever he does to his underlings for not following his rules, no matter how asinine they are."

He had her pinned against the wall in a second, not even aware that he had moved until he was there. He pressed his hardness into her soft flesh, showing her without words what he wanted, needed from her. He pushed his cock into her, once, then again. Tucker kissed her, devouring her mouth, taking her breath away.

"Does this feel like an order to you, Sam? Do I feel like a man who's had enough? I want you, right now. I want to fuck you right here, then I want to take you upstairs and fuck you again, and again."

Tucker pulled her shirt open, ripping the buttons off. Then her shorts were shredded, the jersey material no match for their passion, because as soon as he touched her skin, she began to tug at his clothing as well. His own pants were ripped from him before he could remember he had no other clothes.

As soon as they were both naked, he palmed her ass, lifted, and entered her in one hard push, slamming her back against the kitchen wall. Her legs tightened around his hips, squeezing him closer. His fangs burst through his gums, the anger and need pushing his passions higher.

"Sam, Christ, come for me. Come now!"

He pinched at the point where her shoulder met her neck with his fangs and as soon as her first wave hit her, he bit down, pierced her flesh, and triggered her second climax. She came, screaming out his name as he rode her harder and faster. As soon as she went lax in his arms, he cradled her next to him and strode to the stairs, up through her rooms into the bedroom. His cock still hard and inside of her, Tucker laid her onto the bed, and then rolled to his back, taking her with him.

"Baby, I need you to ride me. Give me all of you. Ride me, Sam; I want you to fuck me."

It took her a moment or two to get rhythm. Each stroke, each time she moved over him, had him surge upward into her.

Her movements were slow and sensual at first, but as he lifted his hips up into her harder and harder, they became frantic with a need to take. Tucker sat up, reached for her nipples, and pulled on first one then the other, her inarticulate sounds driving him closer. He took her hands from his chest and cupped them around her plump breasts, pushing them together for him. When he was satisfied she would leave them there, he sucked hard on one then the other in quick consecution, back and forth. Digging his fingers into her hips to bring her harder down on his cock, he looked up at her.

"Sam, I want you to drink from me. I want to feel your mouth on me, for you to drink from me."

She surged on him. He felt her tighten around him and her eyes darkened to a deep violet color. He had his answer. Pulling his right hand from her, he reached under her pillow where she kept a switchblade, and flicked it open. Never taking his eyes from hers, he sliced an opening across his chest, just where his heart pounded. As he leaned back on his hands, he dropped the bloodied knife over the side of the bed, then lowered himself to his back and waited for her.

His blood running down his chest seemed to be mesmerizing for a few seconds, and then she leaned forward, her breath soft and warm on his chest as she ran her tongue along the thin stream that ran from his abs to the cut. His body reacted to the sensation of her tongue tracing the blood line and had him moaning with anticipation. When she reached the source, she opened her mouth over the wound and sucked. He nearly bucked her off in response, never had anything felt so right. He pulled her arm up from beneath her and put her wrist to his mouth. He bit her deep in the artery there, taking her in as she was him. Their combined climax shattered them, bringing them both to the heavens and then back again.

CHAPTER THIRTEEN

Tucker woke first this time, as it was nearly ten o'clock and he needed to be in shelter before the sun was too much higher in the sky. Tucker was an old vampire and could take sun up to the hottest part of the day. He got up and realized that their clothes, or what was left of them, were still down in the kitchen from last night. She'd be mortified if one of her employees found them there. He materialized to the house he was renting, dressed quickly, then returned to her kitchen. Someone had already picked the kitchen up. He looked around and didn't see anything amiss. Even the trays of flowers were put away. He walked back up to the bedroom just as she was getting up.

"Hi," he told her softly, not wanting to break the quiet of the morning. "I went down to get our clothes and they were gone."

"I...I went down earlier and got them. I...it's not really...they, Sally and Betty, they...they don't need to know my business. Not that they'd mind...I mean, they shouldn't...I got them already. There wasn't much left of...your pants were shredded and, well...I had to...damn it. I'm gonna take a shower, then I have to go to work. I guess you need to leave, or I guess leave again. You didn't bring clothes here, did you? Last night, I mean?"

"No, I didn't." He thought it was funny that she was babbling. "It's all right, baby. I can move through time, sort of transport myself from here to there over great distances. It's my talent, so to speak. And about the pants, that's fine that you threw them out. I'm sure they were a mess." She only nodded and got up, pulling the bed sheet around her.

He watched her. She moved a little stiffly. They had made love several times throughout the night and morning, and as he was a large man, he was sure she was a little tender. He moved to her as she struggled with both the sheet and the door, balancing her and opening the bathroom door for her.

"Here, let me. You don't need to hide yourself from me, Sam. I've tasted nearly every inch of this delectable body, and I love looking at you."

"I'm not comfortable like this. I mean, I know you must think I'm being silly, but I —" He cut her off with a kiss, a kiss that was so gentle and though even in its simplest form, was sensual and heated. When she pulled away and leaned her forehead onto his chest, he held her close, just giving her comfort.

"I don't think you're silly. I think you are a very passionate and vibrant woman who hasn't bared herself, as it were, to anyone and you're shy." He tilted her chin up so that he could look into her eyes still wet with unshed tears. "Don't cry, baby. I won't hurt you. I promise." She nodded again and put her head back on his chest.

He could see her in the mirror over the sink in the bathroom. Tucker pushed the sheet down just enough that he could see the bullet scars well now. He reverently touched the one on her waist, circling it with his fingers. When she stiffened, he nearly stopped, but wanted to reassure her that they didn't bother him.

"Don't, Sam, I want to see. They are a part of you, and they make you who you are. Let me touch them."

He hadn't thought about the bullets going through her, but she had been so small. Where else would they have gone? He touched the second one that was near her spine; another two inches and it would have severed it. The third and fourth were on her right side. Close, he thought. Close to her heart both times. The fifth was low on her belly, and had probably nicked if not gone through her kidney. He shuddered as he thought of the pain she must have been in, even with her mother healing her. He looked for the sixth and didn't see it, but before he could ask, she shifted in his arms, lifted her hands to her hair, and showed him the sixth scar.

"This one he shot last. I didn't feel it. By then I was in so much pain, I couldn't think, let alone realize that he'd shot me again. But it was the one that changed me." The bullet went in just above her right ear and came out the back, near the middle of her skull. "By all rights, it should have killed me instantly; I think my mother had something to do with why it didn't. I was only a weak telepath before, getting a small, very small taste of people's thoughts. After that night, I could feel and hear everything. Then there were the other things. I...they scared me at first...I didn't tell anyone, but it...I could suddenly...one of the things I could do was remember everything. Everything I heard, smelled, touched. Even things I'd read."

"Photographic memory, you have a photographic memory. You said other things. What do you mean? What kind of other things?"

"I can move things by simply thinking about it with telekinesis. It was hard at first, but I got stronger, and the objects got larger, kind of useful now and again. Then there is clairvoyance. I can see things about other people. It...that's how I met Betty. She came into the shop one day. I was running it on my own then, and I got a glimpse of her boyfriend killing her that night, or it turned out to be that night. Anyway, she had come in for a sample and I felt her pain. She had been beaten earlier. So I 'pushed' her into giving me her address and went to her home that night. He had been beating her, and I shot him." He knew that there was probably more to the story than that, but he didn't push her. He just tucked her closer to his body.

"Then there is the psychometric thingy. I can just touch something or someone and tell everything about them or it. I can locate things, lost objects, and people. So long as it hasn't been touched by too many, I can get a reading on things very quickly."

He didn't press when she wouldn't look at him. It was probably easier for her this way. He decided that she would trust him soon enough to face him and herself.

"Who else knows about these abilities?" He worried about her more now. She was a walking lab experiment, and anyone would want to cut her head open and see just what made her the way she was.

"Betty knows, I think. She's never asked, but I know she wonders. But no one else, well, you do. I don't exactly flaunt it, or tell anyone. I know the men in lab coats would have a heyday with me." She finished her thought with a gentle touch into his mind. "I can read your worry, Tucker, as well as your thoughts. I'm not trying to pry, but when you touch me, it's like a direct line to that extrasensory plug-in."

"That's why you don't like to be touched, why you back off when people reach out to you."

"Yes, it's like information overload. Like 'too much information' all in capital letters. That little kid…Lizzy? She felt me pop. It's like we both got a jolt. Most can't feel it but I...she must be a very strong sensitive too."

He could feel the sun bearing down on him even though they weren't near a window. He needed to get below ground. He pulled back from their embrace, and looked down at her. When she smiled at him, his heart flipped over in his chest. Mine!

"I have to go, it's nearly noon. I need to...will you please do me a favor and not go out today? I need to tell you something. It's important, it's...I have a...I need to explain something to you. Will you wait inside for me to return, please, Sam? It's important."

"I need to get these cakes finished today. They're being picked up tomorrow." She stiffened as she spoke. "I won't have time to leave, but I can take care of myself. I've been doing a pretty shitty job of it, but I've managed to not get myself killed all by my lonesome."

"I know, but now that we're mated...I...it could be dangerous for you. Please stay inside. I know its daylight, but there are other creatures that could harm you for...I really need to go. I'll explain tonight, all right?" At her promise to try her very best not to leave the shop, he left. He knew she was giving him the best answer she could under the circumstances.

Instead of going to the rental house, he materialized in the master's mansion kitchen. Duncan, apparently used to people popping in and out, didn't even bat an eyelash as this latest embodiment appeared before him.

"Master Tucker, how nice to see you again. The master and the missus are in the dining room. Would you like for me to announce you?"

"Hummm, no. I need to...I was wondering if I may seek shelter here for the day? I need to talk with my master, but it's too late, I must go to ground. Would you please ask him to…tell him I need to talk with him about something? Something important…it's about Sam, well, Sam and me. Would you please ask him for me?"

Duncan had been around enough vampires in all his lives to know when fatigue from the sun was beating down on one. As he rushed Tucker off to shelter, Tucker was glad for the man and wondered if he would ever find someone so well versed in vampires' needs. Duncan assured him that he would tell the master and the lady of the house.

~~~

"Did he say anything, Duncan, that might give us a clue as to what has happened?" Sara asked as she continued to eat her breakfast. Aaron watched her, only paying about half attention to what Duncan was saying. He was so turned on he hurt. It wasn't until Sara glared at him that he started listening with his entire mind.

"No, missus, he didn't, but he seemed most anxious, if you do not mind my saying so. And he did say it was important. I do hope the young miss is all right. She is quite the baker and I do so love what she can do with sugar."

Aaron thanked Duncan and when he had left, turned to Sara. "Something is wrong. I can feel it. Something to do with Tucker. Can you ask Mel to put a hex on the shop over there to keep Sam safe?"

"Hex? Why you bloodsucking ass! I do not put hexes on things, of all the nerve!" Mel had a habit of coming and going whenever the mood struck her, and apparently today was one of those days. Her anger didn't bother Aaron. He knew she was there with them, Sara's magic blending with his powers to make him incredibly strong mentally. He had said that to aggravate her.

"Why look who's here, and without an invitation too. And for your information, the only ass I'll suck now is Sara's. It is so tasty and sweet." He licked his lips for added effect. Sara stared at him with part amusement and part shock. He laughed harder because of it.

"I really hate you. Really, really hate you, you know that? But I love Sara, and if she wants me to, I'll put a little magic on the place for her. You, my good man, can rot in hell." Mel loved him, Aaron knew this. She had told him that Sara was happy and Mel loved her so she had to love him by default. Aaron went off to rest, wondering how else to irate the Queen of Magick.

CHAPTER FOURTEEN

"Sam, you need to come out front. Right fucking now!"

Sally had her back to the kitchen, staring out into the shop. And Sally never cussed. Sam stood up, moved to the side of the kitchen door just behind Sally, and pulled out her gun. She checked the clip, racked one into the chamber then returning it to the butt of the gun, she hid it behind her, tucking it in the back of her jeans.

"Sally, I want you to move back another step and then two steps to the right. Don't go back in there," Sam whispered calmly to her.

Sam had reached out and knew what was going on. Mr. Hermendez had found her. This was becoming a bad habit, one that she wasn't thrilled about. Someone or something was giving her away.

"He told me to get you and come back. He'll kill the little girl if I don't get you like right now. Sam, I don't want her to die." Her voice was low and full of terror. Sam gave her a tiny push of strength and asked her again to move back.

"You're not. That's it, just a little further. Now turn to your right." When Sally was out of the doorway and up against the kitchen wall, she began to cry. Sam was hurt by the sound, but needed to focus all her energy on the shop and the man there. "I need you to go up to my apartment and call

155

nine-one-one. Tell them we have a hostage situation, all right? You can do this, Sally." Sam took a deep breath when Sally took off toward the stairs.

Sam stepped into the shop and looked around to see where everyone was placed. It was important to know one's enemy. Even if you weren't sure who they were, it was good to know where everyone was. An innocent person could be just as much an enemy as the one holding the gun if one didn't know where they were. If a person miss fired, or the enemy decided to take another life to make a point, knowing all the players would and could save lives.

"Mr. Hermendez, you don't want to hurt her, let her go." Sam had come out with her hands in front of her, palms out and fingers spread. It was a sign of "I'm not armed" and she hoped that he wouldn't shoot her without at least giving her a chance to save the child.

The little girl he was holding looked to be about seven or eight. Her face was streaked with tears and she was sobbing for her mother. Sam had noticed a woman in a crumpled heap on the floor next to the counter and assumed it was her mom. With a tiny touch, Sam assured herself that the mother would heal, but have a nasty headache when she woke.

"I'm the boss here, bitch, not you. I want my kids. You're gonna tell me where they are right now."

He was speaking in English, but it was slurred and broken, spittle spraying from his mouth with each word. He was very drunk, but that didn't make him any less dangerous. In fact, it probably made him more so. He was also very stupid if he thought he was leaving here on his own.

"All right, you can be in charge, but I want you to let the little girl go. You're frightening her. You can take me. I'll come with you to find your wife and kids, just let her go."

Sam was walking toward him. She wanted to make a clean shot if she had to and not let him hurt anyone in the process.

There were seven other people in the shop, not including the girl and her mother. Almost a dozen people to worry about when there were guns, drunks, and anger involved. When Sam started toward the man, Betty, bless her big heart, grabbed the woman on the floor by the ankle and began to drag her behind the massive counter. Once she had her there, she motioned for the others to follow her into the kitchen and safety. She must have made some little noise because before anyone made it to the back, he opened fire. So did Sam.

By the time the police showed up five minutes after Sally called, it was over. Juan Hermendez lay dead. The little girl, Danielle, had a broken arm from being thrown free of him by Sam, and was currently being held by her mother, who had a large laceration at her temple. All the other patrons were fine, if only a little shaken by the ordeal.

Sam was sitting on the floor against the counter bleeding from the bullet she had taken when Juan had turned to shoot Betty. Sam had thrown herself forward, grabbing Danielle's arm with a jerk away from the mad man and been hit almost at the same time she had fired at him. Her shoulder hurt like hell, but she was alive. She was dizzy from loss of blood, not just from the wound, but from her bites from the night before with Tucker.

She knew by all rights she should be dead. His aim had not been off and the bullet should have hit her dead center in the chest right through her heart. She had felt the surge of magic that had propelled her forward a little harder and made her just a little faster in pulling the little girl down and away. She didn't know who had intervened, but she was reasonably sure it wasn't that big vamp's wife, or whatever. She would probably have slowed her down just to be satisfied she was good and shot. No, this was strong magic, but not like her mothers.

David showed up before the ambulance did, but not by much. He had been radioed about a hostage situation and then shots fired at this address almost precisely at the same time. He was just leaving the stationhouse to go home so was able to get there quickly. The coroner was already there waiting for the investigative team to finish with the room. Danielle and Marsha Walsh, members of his brother's pack, were being cared for by Sally and Betty with ice and cold glasses of water. Sam was still sitting on the floor, someone, probably one of the older women, had given her a towel to staunch the bleeding, which had already soaked it through.

"It seems a Mr. Juan Hermendez came in here at approximately two-thirty and took a Miss Walsh, age six, hostage and demanded the proprietor, Miss Sam Hunter, tell him the whereabouts of his wife and children. Miss—"

"I swear to Christ, if you call me 'Miss Hunter' again, I'm gonna stomp your fucking ass. And he didn't want his wife, just the kids. I've told you this story ten times now; the least you could do is repeat it the way I told you."

Sam continued muttering under her breath, something about the officer's parentage and the brain wattage of the combined police force being too low to light a twenty watt bulb. David covered his mouth and coughed to hide the sudden burst of laughter. He had no doubt that she would do just as she had threatened, and he thought Officer Todd did as well, because he looked positively white.

"Has Miss, err Sam been looked at?" He had made the mistake with her name on purpose, just to see her glare at him. She didn't disappoint.

"No, sir, she…well, she won't…that is to say…she's still armed sir. Said she'd only give it to someone of authority. I did try to explain to her that I was the authority and she got nasty with me. I don't think she has much respect for me and the other officers, sir. She did break the gun down and gave me the used clip, but not the weapon itself. I thought that I'd just have an officer secure her until you arrived. It seemed…well, it seemed safer than trying to take it from her. She's a little scary when she's riled."

"You'd better believe I'm scary, you moronic asshole. I swear to Christ, you got your badge from a cereal box, didn't you? Why don't you go and tell your mother, she wants you, and leave me the hell alone? I've had about all I can take of you today." She looked at David and grimaced. "He's a moron."

He looked at the police office and thought maybe Sam wasn't too far off in her estimate. He knelt down in front of her and looked at her wound. She was still bleeding pretty well, but he knew that they wouldn't come close to her while she was still armed. Didn't make them any less stupid, just smart enough to know when to back off apparently.

"Sam, I need your weapon, honey, or I can't let the medical team over here." He held the evidence bag out in front of him, hoping she wouldn't want someone else to take it.

"He's a dumbass, you know that?" She was looking at Officer Todd, not at him. He shifted on his feet slightly to see what he was doing now. Yep, no doubt about it, the man was a moron. He was currently trying to get Betty to leave Marsha alone and to go get in his squad car to be questioned. Betty was gonna hit him in a minute, he just knew it. He turned back to Sam.

He started to say something, but she looked at him. "David, I can't. Let go, I mean. I can't make my hand let go of the butt. He should have killed me. I know where the bullet was headed and it should have hit me in the chest, not in the arm. Someone interfered, someone with magic. I...I feel sick. I wanna throw up, but I can't seem to...my hand. He was intending to kill everyone after he killed me. I had to shoot...I broke that little girl's arm. I heard it snap, the bone just snapped. Can she, you know, do some mumbo jumbo and turn and fix it? Betty was gonna die, I love her, she couldn't die."

Sam didn't know what she was saying, he could tell. She was just emptying her head of every thought that entered it. He saw that she was in shock, and asked someone for a blanket from the ambulance. When they brought it in, he covered her himself and started making soothing noises at her.

He heard her hiss and turned to see Sara and Duncan pushing their way into the room. Sara had a cell to her ear and was shouting to someone on the other end. David nearly laughed at the sight of the two of them, but decided that he didn't want to end up on the wrong end of either of the three in their combined anger.

"I can see her. Yes, she's just sitting there like she hasn't a care in the world. Let me see if I can...hold on, damn it. Here, take this." She shoved a phone at Sam and even David could hear the man shouting at the other end.

He took the phone from Sara and held it to Sam's ear, just knowing it was her mate and that he must have felt her pain. Sam listened for a few seconds, then turned her head away and stared off into the room. He doubted she was seeing or hearing anything. She looked very pale and he could feel her struggling with the pain. He put the phone to his own ear just in time to hear Tucker yelling at her about not letting him in.

"Hello? Is this Tucker? This is Lieutenant Wolff, please calm down and I'll talk to you, or otherwise I'm hanging up this phone." That shut him up.

Tucker took several deep breaths and began again in a much calmer, if not lower voice. David was impressed. His brother would have snarled and demanded that he do as he was told.

"I want to...I need to speak to Sam, please. Can you put her on?"

"I'm sorry, Tucker, but she can't talk to you right now. She's in shock. But I will tell you all I can. She has been shot and has lost a good deal of blood, though I'm sure you can guess why not all of it is from the wound. But she'll be fine. She's also still armed and before you and Sara rile her up again, I nearly had the gun in my possession." David glared at Sara when she snorted. "The medical team won't treat an armed person, and you and Sara have fucked up all progress I've made. I have a dead man here, a little girl with a broken arm, a woman who in all likelihood has a concussion, and the one person who I can help won't let me. Now, if you think you can be a calm and rational person, I'll call you back when I have more information on her health. Until then, back the fuck off." He clicked the phone shut, handed it to Sara, and told Duncan to take her outside of his crime scene or he'd have her arrested too.

Sam had finally passed out. He picked up her weapon by the butt, put it into the evidence bag, and bellowed for the EMTs to get their asses in there now. They worked on her for twenty-five minutes then loaded her onto a stretcher and took her to the closest hospital. She was weak from blood loss, more so than what they could account for, but she would recover. David had an idea why she had lost so much blood just as he had hinted to Tucker, but didn't enlighten them.

"Where are they taking her, David? I'll go with her and have Duncan...is she going to be arrested?"

Sara had calmed down considerably. David was sure she knew more of what had gone down than he would ever know as she had more than likely heard what had happened through her search of the minds of the people there. Sam had saved the lives of everyone in that shop. David knew that as sure as he was standing there. Sara also told him that she had contacted Aaron who relayed the information to Tucker.

"Grant. You should have Reilly meet her there as well. She has mated with that vamp and whatever they do at the hospital, blood work will be drawn. She'll be fine, Sara. She will be arrested initially, but the charges will more than likely be dropped." He looked quickly around the room and then lowered his voice so that just the two of them could hear. "She felt magic intervene on her part. I don't suppose that you might know anything about that, would you?"

Sara nodded before she spoke. "Mel came to me to say that the magic had been breached not ten minutes after she had put it there. I immediately woke Aaron. He hadn't been asleep long. He had asked her to do it and she did it for me. It turned out to be the smartest move he could have made. I think Tucker felt her, and then when she was shot, he dropped to the floor. I can only assume it was Sam's pain he felt as it was happening to her. It was everything Aaron could to do keep him from leaving and going to Sam. He could feel her fear, he said." Sara looked at the bloodied stain on the floor as she continued. "Duncan and I took off immediately to see what we could find out because Sam had blocked Tucker out and he couldn't contact her. I'm not sure now that she was blocking him on purpose. I think she's been doing it for so long that...David, that woman is perhaps one of the bravest women I've ever met."

By the time they were wheeling her out of surgery, it was dusk and Tucker was there to meet David. He wanted to question Sam more, but knew that she needed her mate more than he needed answers. For now. From all accounts, Sam had saved everyone in the shop.

The surgery was a success, the bullet had been removed, and they were pumping her full of fluids. Thomas Reilly made sure she was in a room where he could get his people there to keep an eye on her. Reilly was a vampire, David knew, but he had others, humans that he trusted to take care of his patients when he couldn't. He was on hand to make sure Sam got the best care, and when the time was right and she was released from custody, he would see that she was transferred home into Tucker's care.

David had an officer outside her room to keep her safe. Two armed men in such a short amount of time made him nervous. There was another officer inside the room with her on hand to ask questions when Sam woke up.

He'd had her cuffed to the bed for two reasons. One, she would leave if he hadn't, he was sure of that, and two, she had shot a man…well, two men.

There hadn't been any official word yet, but Sam was being charged with first degree murder in the death of Juan Hermendez until all the facts were gathered. No one believed she'd murdered him, but had only been protecting the people in the shop. By all accounts, Sam was considered a hero, and would more than likely have the charges dropped as soon as it went before a judge.

David went home and after being questioned again by his brother, he went to bed. Just before he closed his eyes, he wondered how she was being located. She had been helping women for some time, David was sure, but over the past few days, she'd had two people try and kill her.

CHAPTER FIFTEEN

When Sam finally opened her eyes eight hours after being brought in, she was disorientated and confused. She remembered the shooting, but very little else that happened afterwards. She moved her arm to test the wound, and was surprised to find the pain wasn't so bad. Her right arm felt heavy, she couldn't move it, and realized it was in a handcuff.

"How are you feeling?" Tucker moved through her mind like a caress and she had to smile, even for a moment.

"Where am I? Oh my God, the little girl, is she all right? I hurt her, Tucker." She started to move off the bed and stopped when he spoke again.

"She's fine, her mother too. Everyone is just fine. You didn't tell me how you're feeling, baby. Are you okay?"

"Just peachy, I guess." She didn't actually hurt all that badly. "My arm doesn't feel so bad. Did you have anything to do with that?"

She could feel his grin. "Yeah, a little. The next time you plan on getting shot, I'll try not to take so much of your blood, that way you'll heal faster. You know I've known you two weeks and you've been shot twice. You do live an exciting life, love."

"I could do with a little less excitement, thank you very much. Why are we mind melding? I can feel you are close."

165

"They won't let me see you but for ten minutes every hour until you wake up, but stay quiet for a little longer." She felt his tension and nearly asked him when he continued. "I have some things I need to tell you so that you aren't surprised. Though with your lifestyle, I'm sure it will be old hat. You're under arrest for now. David seems to think that will go away when it goes before a judge in the morning. Aaron has gotten you an attorney and he is going for justifiable homicide. With all the testimony, it looks good. Sam, I'm sorry. I was so scared when I couldn't reach you and I yelled at you. Can you forgive me?"

"Did you?" She tried to remember those minutes after she'd been shot. "I don't remember. But I didn't know you would be affected too when I was shot. I'm the one who is sorry. Sara. I remember her shoving a phone in my face. Boy that woman is a piece of work. She really hates me."

"I don't think so. She was pretty impressed with how you handled yourself. She sort of has an inside track to people's minds, I guess, kinda like you do. That's why you have an attorney through them; she is feeling guilty about her treatment of you." She felt his hunger then, sharp and hot. "It's almost time for us to come in. Why don't you wake up now for them and we'll be in shortly."

Sam rolled her head to the left and opened her eyes to the officer in the chair. She had to clear her throat twice before he looked up at her. Officer Mason—this one seemed a little more on top of things—said that she was under arrest pending further investigation. He explained how she was not to leave the state, like she could, shackled to the bed like she was, and about the officer outside. When he had read her her rights, he stepped back to allow her visitors time to see her and he could call Lieutenant Wolff, he told her.

~~~

Marta opened her eyes. Something was different. She reached out in the room and found that one of the humans she had brought in the evening before was dead, the other was nearly so. To her, humans were nothing more than food anyway, cattle. There only for her pleasure and food. She didn't even bother with trying to remember who or what they were.

Tucker James. He had finally bonded with his mate. Yes, that was what was wrong. She never thought he'd go through with it. Taking a mate was against her rules. What belonged to her belonged to her until she said otherwise.

Her pet had tried to escape her before and she thought he'd learned his lesson. Apparently not. Well, it was time to bring him home. And when she did, she would drain his mate just to prove to him who was the boss. Oh yes, Tucker was going to learn his lessons and she would be thrilled to teach them to him again.

Closing her eyes, Marta contacted her minion in Ohio. She smiled at his fear. Fear made blood so much richer than that of mere mortals. She wished suddenly that she was there with this man. Drinking from him now would be all the sweeter.

"I take it she has escaped again. You must know that I'm not pleased with your performance. I said for her to be dead, and dead soon." She sent him a small dose of her plans for what his failure was going to cost him. She was thinking she might just kill him anyway for being stupid. "When I give an order, there is no room for stupidity. Kill her," Marta screamed in his mind.

"My lady, she is armed all the time. I've sent two of the men she has wronged, but she has taken them both without any problems. And this time there was..."

"There was what? Did Tucker help her? He'd better not have had the opportunity. I told you only during sunlight. If you've fucked this—"

"No! No, my lady." She loved his fear. "It's during the day, I swear it. Today, as a matter of fact. The news is running it all the time. No, my lady, it was a surge of power. Magic. More than I've ever felt before. More than you have—"

"No one is stronger than me," she shouted through their link. "I will know who dares to interfere in my work. You'll find this person and bring them before me. And I'll...no, it's time I brought my Tucker home. I'll be there soon. You'll make sure that I'm welcomed in the way befitting me."

The connection closed, but not before she felt his terror. Smiling, she sat back down on her bed, thinking. It was time to bring Tucker home, past time really. He would pay for this, pay for making her angry. And so would that interfering woman he thought to replace her with. No one, not even a mate, would take Marta's place in Tucker's life. She had made him. He was hers and hers only.

She rose from the massive bed and summoned someone to come and clean up the mess. Dead bodies were not her problem. Cleaning them up and disposing of them was not her job. She was master. There were plenty more cattle around when she needed them and didn't give another thought to the dead bodies strewn about the room.

Marta was an older vampire, but not nearly as old as some masters. She had come into her power position by good, old fashioned lying, cheating, and black magic. She had killed more than two hundred mage, witches, and other magical beings and had absorbed their power base. Whenever she felt one enter her territory, or one was close enough, she would hunt them down and kill them. The added strength and energy they gave her kept her strong and feared. She ruled with an iron fist and a heavy hand, killing the strong as well as the weak and smashing the ones who got into her way. She often used sex, or what she considered sex, as a punishment. To her, they were one and the same.

Tucker was hers and she'd have him back. She couldn't wait to tie him back to her bed. Just thinking about the gorgeous, superbly well-formed man made her wet with need. He could make her come more and harder than anyone else. Yes, it was time to bring him home. She reached out and summoned him, knowing full well that he wouldn't answer. It was like a game to her, one that she had no doubt she would win.

CHAPTER SIXTEEN

Tucker came into her room and went directly to the bed and kissed Sam. He had never been so happy to see anyone in his entire existence. The kiss might have gone on longer had Aaron not interrupted him with a gentle but firm push.

"Hi," Tucker said. Sam was embarrassed, but he didn't care. He just realized he loved her, he loved her very much.

"Hi yourself. They said I was under arrest and that I couldn't leave here." Sam spoke to the room in general, but kept stealing glances at him. Tucker sat on her bed and pulled her onto his lap. He laughed when she struggled, but he was stronger and she was still slightly weak from all that had happened to her.

"I'm taking care of that," Aaron told her. "I have hired you a lawyer and he'll have you released into my custody by tomorrow afternoon. Duncan will come and get you and bring you to my home. We can care for you there, and Tucker will be able to see you." Tucker hadn't asked, but apparently Aaron had done so anyway.

"I don't think so. I have a business to run." Sam looked at him then at Aaron. "I need to be there. Thanks, but I think under the circumstances, I'd like to be at my home. Beside, before you make arrangements like that you should really clear it with your...mate? She doesn't particularly care for me and I'm pretty sure she'd be pissed about me being there. I know I'm not real thrilled about being there."

"Sara is the one who suggested it. Besides, it's a moot point. You're coming and that's all there is to it." Tucker nearly laughed at Sam's expression, but thought he might live longer if he didn't. "My way is law with my vamps and I can't care for you or see to your wellbeing if you aren't close." Tucker felt Sam tense in his arms and tried to pull her back. He wondered if there would ever be a time when these two got along.

"Does that tone usually work for you? 'Cause I gotta tell ya, it doesn't do a thing for me." Sam sat up in the bed and poked Aaron in the chest with her finger. "I don't need you or anyone else 'seeing' to me. I'm a big girl and have been on my own, taking care of myself for a long time. So, Mr. High and Mighty, fuck off."

Aaron just grinned at her. Even though Tucker didn't know the master well, he could tell that this particular grin was not one he'd consider friendly. Maybe even a little scary. Sam looked as though she could give as good as she got. Tucker smiled and admitted only to himself that he was very proud of her.

"I see. Well how about this then, Sam it would please me greatly if you were to come and be a guest in our home." His tone was sugary sweet. "You will need to heal for a few more days. And as you know, you've lost a great deal of blood and have been shot twice now. I think it would be very beneficial and wise of you if you were to come so that your mate, Tucker, could be with you and you two could use this time to get to know one another." He paused, then, "Nah, I like 'my way is law' much better. Duncan will be here in the afternoon to collect you. Someone will go to your apartment and pack you a few belongings as well. I am master of this realm and as my newest subject, you will obey."

Aaron just stared at Sam and before either could say anything to either of them, Tucker felt someone enter his mind.

He stiffened and stood up. He looked around the room as though he felt someone's presence. He looked at Aaron. Tucker didn't need to try and figure out who had invaded his mind with an iron fist. Marta. His mind seized up and his heart began to pound. He started to back away from Sam's bed.

"Stop! What is it? You'll tell me now, Tuck, is it her? Is she summoning you back? Answer me, damn it!" Aaron was sounding frantic, but Tucker could barely focus.

"She calls," Tucker gasped out. "She is demanding that I return to her posthaste. And that I bring Sam with me. I cannot go, sire, she will kill her. It is forbidden for me to kill my maker and I will if she tries to harm Sam."

Tucker was afraid to look at Sam so he watched Aaron pulled his cell phone out and called Thomas, and then he called to his mate. He needed Sam at the estate immediately and with Sara clouding everyone's mind, and Thomas taking care of the paperwork, she would be gone within the hour, he told someone over the phone.

"What is it, Tucker, what's happening?" Sam's voice was as gentle as her touch. "Who is she, your wife? I don't understand what's happening."

Sam was scared for him. Tucker could feel it. His fear, his hatred for his maker was tangible and he wished again that he had just left when he'd realized what Sam was to him.

"She's my maker. She turned me. She is calling me back to her side and you with me. It is her right to demand, and I...I don't...Sam, I cannot take you with me. She will kill you."

"No one is going anywhere. As soon as Duncan arrives, we're leaving. And Sam, I'd very much appreciate it if you'd just cooperate. I don't have time to explain now, but you should know that I will do what I need to keep you both safe. I don't like doing this, but I will command you if you don't."

"You know, asking someone to do something might go a lot longer toward getting cooperation than fucking acting like you're the only one who can fix things," Sam snapped. "I'm not stupid and I don't appreciate you treating me like it."

"You're right. I'm sorry." Aaron took a deep breath. "Please, let's just get you both at the mansion and we'll explain everything. Tucker is in trouble and he's come to me for help. You were an added bonus none of us expected. I swear I will explain things when we are somewhere safe."

Duncan and the large Hummer arrived thirty minutes later. No one seemed to notice or care that Sam was being escorted out of the building by Tucker, two very large men and one small, dapper man. Colin Larimore, a friend and master of his own realm, had come to help with the escape. Sam was thankfully silent as they moved from hospital to car. But when they got to the house, she started to protest again. Tucker pulled her into his lap.

"I don't see what this has to do with me. I didn't do anything to the bitch...yet anyway. Where does she get off demanding anything of anyone for that matter? It must be in the genes, that's it. Are all vampires stubborn pains in the ass?" This last was asked just as Tucker carried her into the house.

"Mostly, yes they are," Sara said with a great deal of humor in her voice. "In fact, now that you mention it, most bakers are as well, I've noticed. However, sometimes they are correct when they bully us, not so much with the bakers. Welcome to my home again, Miss Hunter. I don't believe you've ever come through the front door on your own before. Must be a novel experience for you."

Sara was waiting for them to return in the open area of the great stairs.

"To be honest, I'm not really on my own now." Sam glared at him when Tucker set her down. "Well, it's been very...hummm enlightening, but I got places to go and people to meet." Sam turned to leave and walked into Tucker's large chest. "Tucker, I have to go home. I don't belong here."

"You're mine, Sam. You do belong here. You belong where I am and I, you. Come with me, we need to talk. Sire? I need to talk to all of you, if you please?"

He took her hand and they both followed the master and Sara into the living room. There was a nice fireplace that had a very low but warm fire. Everyone took their seats. Only Tucker stood.

"Sam and I have mated and now my maker is demanding that I return to her and bring my mate with me," he started in a rush. "She is a horrible being who lives off the misery of those she commands. I came here because I had heard about what you as master had done for Dominic Marshall. Most of us have waited for someone like you for nearly all of our lives and had hoped to have you petition for my release. I have...I had a great many things to bring to you; I have many talents as an older vampire. I have many abilities that older ones do not. But I cannot bring this to your realm. Had I only myself to ask, I would, but I have a mate now. I would ask that you please accept my offer from before, and care for Sam. I will return to Marta this evening. You are a great leader among our kind." He started to leave, to take Sam with him to the lair and spend the night making love to her, but she had other things in mind. And she spoke before Aaron could.

~~~

"Who the hell do you think you are?" Sam had had enough of these people telling her what was best for her. "You think that because we had a good time in the sack you can just dump me with a bunch of strange bloodsuckers and saunter off into the sunset? No offense, Mr. Master Person." She directed this last bit to Aaron, who was doing everything in his power not to burst out laughing. Why, she couldn't tell, but waited for his answer. Sam had Tucker backed up against the wall and was punctuating each word with a sharp poke to his chest. She was going to have her say, damn it.

"Oh I assure you, none taken."

With a nod, she continued. "I may not take my lunch from someone's neck, but I do have resources to take care of myself, and you as well if I have to, you stupid jerk. If you think for one second that I'm gonna just be the type of woman who says, 'oh my, take care of me you big brute of a man,' honey, you so don't know me."

She turned to glare at Colin who was literally rolling on the floor, tears streaming down his cheeks he was laughing so hard. Shade, his mate, Sam had been told, was stuffing a couch pillow in her face and making weird gulping noises. Aaron and Sara were leaning on each other, trying very hard not to look like they were laughing, but only succeeded in making themselves look constipated.

"What's wrong with you people?" she asked the room. She didn't understand these beings. She was trying to be serious and make the stupid man understand she didn't need him or anyone else for that matter, and they were laughing. This was obliviously vampire humor and beyond her understanding. As she turned to go, Tucker scooped her up in his arms, and with a raised brow to Aaron, he took her to the sublevels and the rooms he had been given.

"I think you need —"

His mouth was covering hers, taking her, tasting her. He began pulling at her clothes. First, the shirt came off, which didn't fare any better than the one before. He was dipping his head down to her bare breasts and pulling one deeply into his mouth, tormenting her erect nipple with his tongue. When she had left the hospital, no one had brought her anything of her own to wear home. She was wearing something Tucker had brought her from Shade, he'd told her. Sam hoped that Shade hadn't been too terribly attached to them as there were now in shreds.

She could feel her body responding to his sensual assault. Her pants were suddenly too tight, too heavy. She wanted to touch him, needed to feel his skin against her.

"Tucker, please, I need...I need something more."

She tore at his shirt, ripping the material as if it were no more than tissue paper, need giving her strength she had no idea she had. When she had it off, she leaned forward and took his hard nipple into her mouth and bit him, bit him hard, drawing a small drop of blood to the surface. He reached behind her to her pants and buried his hands down into them, pulling her up to his cock, which was hard and hot against her soft folds. She wrapped her legs around him, and held on while riding him up and down his cock with the power of her legs.

He started toward the bed, but she needed him now. When he stopped and pulled her legs from his hips and slid her down his body, she started pulling at his belt. He moved her hands, dropped to his knees in front of her, and yanked her pants off quickly. He buried his mouth against her pussy and sucked her into his mouth, panties and all. She screamed out as the sensations of what he was doing to her pulsed through her body. When Tucker lifted her leg, positioned it over his shoulder, and tore the material from his goal, she grabbed a handful of his hair and held on. Her pussy gushed with her cream; a small trickle of it ran down her thigh. More of her juices gushed as his head lowered to her.

Tucker lapped at her, even as he inserted a finger into her heat. He once again tongued her clit, and suckled it. When she started moving against his fingers and his mouth, he inserted a second, then third into her. She was close to coming and he'd not even entered her yet.

"Baby, I want to feed from you. I want to feed from you pussy. Let me bite you, taste you." He teased her clit, driving her closer to the edge.

"Yes, oh God, Tucker. Bite me, feed from me." Her knees weakened at the thought of him biting her there. Biting her and drinking from her.

The pain was immense but over quickly. It was replaced by the most intense orgasm she had ever had. When he drew her clit and her blood into his mouth and swallowed, she came again, still rocking from the first one. Her knees buckled now and had he not lowered her to the floor, she would have fallen. He never stopped and before he licked the small wound to seal it, Sam had come four more times. But he wasn't finished with her yet.

Tucker leaned back on his heels, her cum and juices glistening on his chin and lips, and stroked his engorged cock. The blood filled head was as big as a large plum. The tip was leaking cum, and the desire to taste him overwhelmed her. She sat up quickly and reached for him, taking him into her mouth before he could stop her, not that he could have. When he started gently fucking her hot wet mouth, she moaned.

He started to pull away, but she growled at him. He pushed harder into her, not being gentle now. Suddenly, he jerked her away by grabbing a handful of her hair and turned her around. While she was up on her hands and knees, he rammed his cock deep into her pussy. He pulled out nearly to the tip and rammed into her again. Again and again, he'd pull out just to the head and slam hard into her. Reaching around to her pussy, he pinched the small exposed piece of flesh, leaned down, bit her on the shoulder, and came, jerking and pulsing in her hard over and over until he dropped on top of her, her own climax still singing through her body.

Long minutes passed before she moved. Even longer before she could gather any strength to think about how much pain they would be if they slept on the floor. But Tucker picked her up and carried them both to the bed. He slid her in under the sheets and joined her. Sam never moved, even after he pulled her body to lay across his. She lay just the way he put her, exhausted and sated. They both slept throughout the rest of the night and all through the next day.

Their rest was complete, their bond as well. Sam wasn't sure how she knew this, but she did. They were a couple and would very much need each other in ways they would never have thought possible. Marta had come for them.

CHAPTER SEVENTEEN

Sam was sitting in the kitchen when Sara walked in at two o'clock the next afternoon. Sara looked at Duncan with a raised brow as if to say, "what's going on" and he shrugged his shoulders.

"She has been sitting there for a few hours now, missus, and not said a word in all that time." Duncan's voice was low. "I have tried to speak to her, but she does not seem to making any sense, so I stopped trying. I'm very worried for the young miss."

Sara knelt down in front of her and touched her chin. "Sam, what is it? What's the matter? Did you and Tucker have a fight?"

Sam stared at her for a minute, then two, looking as if she didn't or couldn't see her. Sara gently reached out and hit the wall Sam always had up. Sara looked around the room and saw that the shades were drawn tight against the house and she reached for Aaron.

"Something's wrong with Sam. She seems to be in a trance or something. I can't reach her. I'm worried, Aaron. What if that woman has her and is hurting her?"

"How long has she been like that?" Aaron was asleep, not really needing to wake to speak to her. He was her mate, her love, and they could talk always.

"Duncan said about two hours. He said that he tried talking to her, but she doesn't make sense when she answers. Her eyes are open, but she seems to have stepped out. What do you think I should do?"

"I'm coming, love, but call Mel or one of the others. Maybe they can feel something you can't."

When Aaron entered the kitchen, Eliz and Mel were arguing about something, no doubt Sam's problem. Sara wanted to smack them all.

"I didn't say that. I said I think she's meditating. You're the one who said she was in a trance." Mel's voice had a tone, tempered a little because of who she was talking to, but a tone nonetheless.

"What I said, you blockhead, was that she is searching for something or someone, not a trance. Keep up, you dolt. I swear, sometimes I wonder if you weren't switched at birth. There isn't any way Savannah gave birth to someone as stubborn as you are." Elizabeth huffed at Mel. "I don't even know where you got that. I'm not stubborn. A granddaughter should be more circumspect of their elders, not a bitch."

"Circumspect of what? I haven't zapped her, have I? I call that being very circumspective." Sara started laughing at Mel, but caught herself. "And stop calling me names. You're not very good at it anyway. You're dating yourself with 'blockhead.' It's so sixties, the nineteen-sixties, that is. How many does that make for you now, a hundred, maybe a thousand?"

"Good morning, ladies," Aaron said as he walked in the room. "So, we're fighting again, are we? Always a pleasure with you two. You make things seem so...oh I don't know, tense isn't quite the word I'd use, but I think you get it. Have we figured out anything other than we are all incredibly old?" He gave each woman a peck on their cheek. He dearly loved her family, but they could be hard on the nerves at times. Sara wanted to bash their heads in.

"I think she's trying to sort something out." Eliz stated happily, and turned and stuck her tongue out at her granddaughter. Sara burst out laughing. "The girl has a very tight rein on her mind, and even I couldn't break in. Well, I probably could, but I didn't want to hurt her trying. Poor thing. Someone should probably wake her mate up."

Mel just growled at her grandmother. She was getting really good at it, too, Sara realized. Mel had heard Aaron growl at her once and Mel had decided she liked the effect it had on people. When she had done it in her Court once, the entire guard took a step back from her. Sara still got a tickle out of the look on Mel's new head guard's face. They had been terrified beyond belief. Sara didn't have the same effect on Aaron since he was much better at it than her.

"I...she's trying to remember something she forgot. She is...her momma is talking to her. I can hear them. She's sad for her." Everyone turned around to look at Mac. He was standing just inside the kitchen door, his backpack still strapped to his little back, jacket in hand.

"You can hear her talking with her mother, Mac?" Sara looked at Aaron and he picked his son up. "Do you know what they're saying, son?"

"Her momma is gone, but she needed to tell Sam somethin', somethin' important, she said, so I brought her to Sam. She said she wouldn't hurt her, that Sam needed her. I...she said she was Sam's momma and I know how much I need my momma, so I brought her to Sam. Was that all right?"

"He's a necromancer. My...my mom said that he's a necromancer because of the circumstances surrounding his birth. Mom...my mom said that he was...he nearly died before he was born and one of his gifts is the ability to raise or talk with the dead. She said he'll be very powerful one day." Sam had tears in her eyes.

Sara reached out and hugged Sam. If anyone needed it, she did. Then she realized what Sam had said. A necromancer, her son was a necromancer. Sara sat down hard in one of the kitchen chairs. She could only stare at Sam then her son. He was a warlock. He would be able to...she didn't know what he'd be able to do, but right now, he could talk with the dead.

"No, Mrs. MacManus, not a warlock, he's a wizard vampire, a very rare breed of both. He will be a great man among his people, and greatly respected as both a vampire and as a wizard. He will live many centuries and do many great things. His own mate will be someone of great wealth, but I don't know of what. They will bring you both many descendants."

"You...you can see this, his future?" Aaron asked.

"Yes. It's one of the things I can do. Lizzy too will be respected; her mate will be one of the few men you will like in her life. Her son will conquer evil in a way that will have repercussions for many a millennium. Lizzy has already met her future mate."

"Who...how do you...I don't understand, how can you know this?" Sara was reeling, her head and mind trying to process what she had just been told.

"I just can. I don't know why. My mom, I guess. Maybe the...maybe something else. It's why I don't like to be touched. I'm a telepath and an empath. Well, that and more, but that's not important. Mom said that I need to call the Courts of Magick and demand that the vampire that torments Tucker be brought before them. Do you know who they are?"

"Yes, it's these two and a few others." Sara pointed to Mel and Eliz. "They hold the magic that everyone uses within them. Mel is the reigning queen, the Mistress of Light, Keeper of Magic. The other woman is her grandmother and the first queen. They're true immortals, in that they can't be killed."

"I don't remember the last time a mortal called forth a Courts of Magic, I wasn't even aware that you knew about it. Did she tell you what they are, and what they do?" Elizabeth had been created, not born. She was created to procreate a successor to take over when she decided to leave, and to watch and maintain all magic, dark and white. She had created the Courts to govern all species, so that no one group could harm another.

"Yes, she said that the Courts of Magick was made up of nine beings, the queen and her champion, and someone from each race, and never the same group of nine." Sam shook her head as she continued. "When someone calls them, they assemble in a neutral place whether in this realm or the queen's, and hear both sides of the claim for and against the magic used. She also said that what they decided was law and bond over to immediate fulfillment, sort of the judge, juror and executioner. I just don't understand what sort of magic his maker used against Tucker and why it would be beneficial to go before them. But my mom said I'd figure it out soon."

"All is magic and magic is all. Stupid, I know, but it basically means that everything is based on magic and the belief in it. Vampires use magic, although some don't believe it's magic." Sara made a pointed look at Aaron, who still believed that he just was and it had nothing to do with powers of magic. At his look of profound innocence, she continued. "But the fact that they can live, and live for a great number of years off of blood, just screams magic. I don't know what Tucker suffered at her hands, but if it involved her vampirism, then she is subject to the laws as well as anyone else."

"So, how does one call a meeting? Who approaches whom? Marta is getting close, so we need to make these decisions now," Aaron said. He never put Mac down, but held him close. Sara knew how he must feel.

"She's close," Sam said. "She's very close. Mom said that she may be in your territory sometime tonight."

~~~

Marta moved along the perimeter of the MacManus estate, watching and waiting. She could feel the hum of the electricity, but didn't know enough about it to figure out its source. She only knew that is was a security system, a good security system. Still, she was virtually impossible to see with the shadows pulled tight around her. Raising her face to the air, she took a deep breath and found what she wanted. Flashing forward, she was upon them before they knew it.

"Are you sure no one can find us here?" The voice was young; Marta loved it. "My mom will spill her guts if she finds out that I'm smoking."

Marta smiled. She loved the taste of fear in the blood. It gave it a spice that she had grown to crave over the centuries. Then there was wolf blood, young wolf blood…she was going to dine well tonight.

"That's why we're doing it out here, stupid, so we don't get caught." This voice was older, but not much. And still a wolf. "You can be such a baby at times. Come on, I hid everything over here."

The two teenage wolves were walking across the deep, dark woods. Marta thought they smelled fresh, clean. Soap and the sweet smell of innocence was all around them. They moved to a small clearing just down from the falls. Marta could also smell sex, though not from these two. It was in the grasses and the very air. Different scents of different people. But they mattered little to her; she wanted the ones that were fresh.

Once they gotten their cigarettes out and lit, they sat down and watched the waterfall. After ten minutes had passed, Marta struck at the youngest boy. He dropped his smoke as he just suddenly disappeared. One second he was there, and then he was gone. Marta laughed when she had him, knowing the other boy's terror.

"Jase," the boy whispered. "Are you there? Come on, buddy, I won't call you a baby anymore."

Marta laughed out loud.

~~~

Davey sniffed the air, hoping to find…the smell assaulted his scenes immediately, making him gag. Blood and lots of it. As he started to move home, he felt something hit him hard across the middle. The pain was incredible. He put his hand to the area and felt a wet, sticky substance on it. He was hurt, his blood covered his hand, and it was then that he felt it soaking his pants around the top. He curled his arm around himself and took off running. He needed to shift, but it took someone as young as him a lot of concentration to do it. But he couldn't stop, not now. Something was chasing him; something was trying to kill him.

"Don't you wanna play little boy?" the voice asked. "I so love a good game of chase. Hurry, hurry, I don't want this to be too quick."

He heard the woman's voice; it seemed to echo all around him, inside of him. Davey ran faster, tripping and staggering over roots and rocks. Terror made him forget that he could see much better than anything else in the forest. When something, he assumed it was her, hit him again, he fell to the earth, gasping for breath. She had hit is face this time, breaking his jaw and shattering his left eye in the socket, knocking his eye from his head.

He got up and started forward again, weak from loss of blood and from pain. He was disoriented and confused, not knowing which way home was. He wanted his mom; he wanted her to hold him, to tell him it was all right, he was going to be all right.

"Poor baby wants his mommy," she taunted him. "Too bad, little boy. She's not going to be able to help you now. You're mine." And with that, the woman stepped in front of him, grabbed him by the throat, and ripped, tearing his jugular out.

Davey dropped to the ground, his life's blood draining from him and saturating the forest floor. The last thing he saw before he died was the woman rubbing his blood over her body and dancing in the puddles beneath him.

CHAPTER EIGHTEEN

When Bradley and the others first came upon the scene, he dropped to his haunches and bayed to the moon, calling to the others Davey had been found. Davey March had been tortured and killed, and it hadn't been an easy death either. Bradley, careful to stay out of the blood trail, moved along the path that Davey had taken, trying to get away from his attacker. He could see where it had hit him the second time, slicing open his face and tearing away the tissue and his eye. When he got to the first hit, he could smell bits of his bowel, where when whoever had hit him had torn through his stomach and disemboweled him, spilling his intestines from his frame. Davey had never stood a chance.

When more of the pack arrived, Daniel, one of the men with him, had already shifted and was gathering evidence for David when he got there. He had worked with him before, and knew what to look for. David being the local police helped keep a lid on things that happened that no human would understand.

"Have you found Jason yet? I understand from Patty, his mom, that they were together." Bradley was hurting. He had known these two since they were pups, and now one of them was dead.

"No, I was hoping Jase might be close, but I haven't picked up anything yet. Besides, I didn't want to leave him alone." They weren't afraid of the forest animals bothering his body, but stayed out of respect for his kind. Pack took care of pack.

"I'll have a look around and see what I can find. I'll take Peter and Jacob with me." Bradley shifted again and summoned the other two men to follow.

It was still a good three hours before sunrise, and ten since the boys had managed to sneak out of their homes. Bradley hoped that Jason March, cousin to Davey, was still alive, but looking down at the young man's body, he didn't hold out much hope.

Thirty minutes later, they found him. Jason was still alive, but barely. He had been tied to a tree upside down by his feet. He was naked and his flesh was scored with hundreds of knife wounds that all dripped into a puddle beneath him. Bradley quickly shifted into human form and grasped him around the waist, unmindful of their shared nudity. Peter managed to get the rope untied from his feet and they slowly lowered him to the ground, careful not to lay him in his own blood. Bradley carried him to a clearing, just north of the falls.

"Contact Sheila and tell her to bring the med team, but do it without alerting the others." Bradley looked down at the boy. "I want everyone to be on their toes and coming to Jason could cause someone to get hurt."

"Alpha?" Jason's voice was weak and barely above a whisper. But Bradley heard him. He leaned down to quiet him, to calm the young pup.

"Shhhh, hush now, I've got you. You're going to be all right. Help is on the way." Bradley, using his fingers as gently as he could, wiped some blood off of Jason's face.

"She said I had to...I'd die if I didn't...tell you. I...she said Tucker, Tucker is hers. That she wants him...he has to go home. Kill more...if...she will kill my mom if he won't." Jason gave his message to Bradley and slid into a deep sleep of the very weak. His pulse was thready and weak. His blood pressure was low. He would be lucky if he made it through the night, Bradley thought.

He held onto the young cub until the medical team arrived. Pack had their own medical services. It was just too difficult explaining to humans how their kind healed quickly and sometimes, well, most always explaining that if a hurt or injured were shifted, they would be completely healed. No, it was just easier to have some on hand for just such emergencies. As he walked away, he called Aaron.

"We found the other one, he's alive. Barely. But I have a message for one of yours, for Tucker. Is he there by any chance?" Bradley felt tears fill his eyes as he spoke to Aaron.

"No, not with me, but I can contact him. Would you like for me to send him to you? I believe he is with a group of searchers in the South. I believe the person in charge of his group is Alice Manner. Does that help?"

"Yeah, I can contact her." Bradley reached out to her as her alpha. "Can you meet me at the pack house? We need to talk. This concerns one of our kind now. And now that she's involved me and mine, I want revenge."

~~~

"When was the last time you saw him?" Bradley just walked in the door to the Pack House as Aaron asked about his man.

Tucker had been missing for nearly three hours when they'd been alerted, and it was well into daylight. Bradley had seen what the woman, Marta, had done to the two young wolves, and what she would do to Tucker was too horrific to think about. Bradley knew that Aaron had told Sam, although they both figured she was just as aware as they were. Aaron was frantic with worry.

"I have twenty-five wolves searching the grounds for him, and another ten going over the security tapes. Pete is in there now going over all the electrical lines, seeing which ones may have been breached. I don't know what else we can do at this point." Bradley had just left the infirmary, looking in on Jason who was going to make it, thanks mostly to the sips of vampire blood now running through his system. "We'll find him, Aaron."

Bradley hoped so. He didn't know what do to about Sam. She was too calm, Bradley had been told, scary calm.

~~~

When Tucker woke up, he was chained by silver links to the wall of a large cave by both his feet and legs. His bare body was covered in cuts, mostly superficial, but others were very deep. Marta was trying to weaken him by slowly draining him of his blood; this was something he knew she did as a final punishment. What she would do to him then, he didn't want to think about. He reached out to Aaron, and realized that he couldn't get past the tight magic surrounding the cave.

"The cave is nice, isn't it, sweetheart? I just love the deep walls and the nice pool. We could bathe in it later if you'd like." She sounded…she almost sounded normal, but when one looked at her, madness stared back from her black eyes. Tucker was suddenly very afraid.

"Why are you doing this? I want you to let me go, Marta. I have a mate now and we can't be together ever again. I can't feed from you either. You have to let me go." He tried for a calm, reassuring voice; he didn't want to anger her any more than he needed to.

"Why, you know I can't let you go. You're mine, Tucker, and I love you. You always have been mine, and always will be." She flashed to his side, jamming a blade into his side to the hilt. "And if I can't have you, lover boy, then no one will." She twisted the knife hard, and then pulled it out, the blood pouring from the fresh wound. Tucker lost consciousness again.

He woke sometime later and tried to reach out to Sam, then Aaron. He couldn't seem to break through. He was so weak by now that he couldn't stand up. The silver from the chains was digging into the flesh of his wrists and ankles. He heard a noise and turned to look at his maker.

"You can't contact them, I've warded the walls. They can't find our little love nest either. I have thought of everything so no one will interrupt us during our special time together."

The cave was different now, he noticed. There was a large bed, draped in long, sheer curtains and a comforter was thrown over it. Rugs were spread all over the dirt floor, heedless of the insects crawling over and under them. There were pictures of people he didn't know, and doubted that she did either. Some of them had been torn from newspapers others were old and yellowed. There was a large stuffed chair with a pillow on it, several more strewn around the floor. Near the pool of water there was a fire pit with a large fire burning in the circle with even more pillows stacked around it. Candles were everywhere, on every available surface, in every conceivable color and smell. If it hadn't been so pathetic, it might have been romantic.

"Where did this stuff come from?" He asked. "Did someone bring it to you?"

Tucker hoped someone had and they would report what they'd seen. But his hopes were dashed with her answer.

"Oh, I made it, isn't it beautiful?" She flitted around the room in a teddy and heels.

Marta looked as if she hadn't been feeding well. Her skin was pasty and dry, her bones sticking out hard at odd angles. She had always been plump, heavier than the woman of today, but more to the style of the ones during their time as humans. Tucker shuddered when he thought of her trying to feed from him.

"Marta, I don't know why you're doing this. I can't feed from you. You are not my mate. You know that, don't you?" He tried again to reason with her, but she just ignored him.

If a mated vampire fed, or tried to feed from someone other than his mate, the blood would poison him. Not killing him necessary but eventually it would drive him to insanity and to the sun. That was why mates, vampire mates, only had one true love, the one that would be with them throughout eternity. If needed, a vampire could feed from his master, but that too would make a vampire ill.

"I must go now, love," she told him. "I need to build my strength so that I can be able to feed you later. I must take care of mine. I was thinking that we should have a child, you and I. Wouldn't she be beautiful? My looks and your...well, she would be so beautiful." She left him hanging there, and he fell into a weak and troubled sleep, too scared to think about what she would do if she found Sam.

Marta returned sometime later. He didn't know when or what time it actually was. He was so disorientated that he didn't know if he had been there for ten hours or ten days. His energy was draining away and it wouldn't be long before he would be too weak to even feed. His need for Sam was growing exponentially; he needed to touch her both in mind and in body. Seeing her again was what kept him from just giving up and giving in to Marta.

"Let me go, Marta, please. I'm not going to live if you—"

She rushed at him. "You'll live. You'll live because I command you to. As your maker, I command you to live." Her laughter was manic, terrifying. "You don't want to make me angry, Tucker. You know how I—"

A being shimmered into the cave. It was a creature he had never seen before, but had heard of. It was a centaur, a beautiful creature of half man and half horse. Tucker closed his eyes, thinking he had surely gone over the edge, but when he opened them again, there he still stood.

"Marta Lipscomb," he said. "You are hereby ordered to appear before the Courts of Magic. You are to appear at seven o'clock this very evening, and you will be ready for trial. The prisoner, a Tucker James, will be brought with you as well. Do you have any questions?"

"I...what is the Courts of Magi? Am I being awarded for my abilities?" The girly squeal in her voice hurt Tucker's head. He didn't know what was going on and he didn't care. Someone had found him.

"The Courts of Magic, and I'm not privileged to know the ins and outs of the Courts. I am just the Summoner. Do you have any more questions?" At her negative reply, the centaur disappeared magically, leaving a scroll with the pertaining information behind as to where to go and the time.

Tucker stared at the place where the creature had been and couldn't wrap his mind around it. He had heard what he had said to Marta, but it as yet hadn't registered in his overtaxed mind. Courts of Magic? Mel, the queen was summoning them to—

"Oh Tucker, we are going to court! Isn't that grand? I bet they have heard of the good things I've done for our kind. Yes, that's it. I'll be getting something from the queen. I'm so excited. Oh, what should we wear?"

Dresses began to appear. Dozens at a time in as many colors as there were styles. Then clothing for a man appeared as well—shoes and belts, coats and ties. Tucker felt himself weaken more. This couldn't be happening; Marta surely couldn't be rewarded for her "good" deeds.

At six forty-five, they materialized in the main hall of one of the outer realms estates. Tucker had heard there were several from the human world and wondered briefly where they were. The one that they were entering was made specifically for them, and would seal closed as soon as they entered, never to open again, the scroll had said. Because they had been expected, the guard was there when they arrived. There was a company of ten royal guards there to meet them.

Marta was so happy. She felt like royalty herself, she'd told him over and over. She had allowed Tucker to bathe in the pool and had given him what she considered suitable clothes for court appearance. He was clad in an outfit straight out of the sixteenth century, powdered wig and all. He could barely walk, much less stand.

The guards shouldered Tucker's weight, nearly carrying him when he fell into them several times. He had tried to apologize to them, but they never said a word. When some led Marta to the large chamber, others took Tucker in the opposite direction Marta was being led. Marta didn't even notice he was taken from her, her thought only on how she could manage to live in such splendor someday soon. He was glad for her distraction.

CHAPTER NINETEEN

There was a long table with several beings sitting at it. The queen and her champion, Elizabeth, Mel's grandmother. The other seven were a varied group of magical and thought to be mythical creatures, including another centaur. In addition, there were what seemed to be several hundred people and beings scattered around the room. None of the inhabitants of the room were dressed as Tucker and Marta were, just wearing everyday street clothes, though neither would have noticed.

Mel was now Melody, Mistress of Light, Keeper of Magic, and her duty in these proceedings was to read the charges against the accused. She had never relished a job so much, as she too had seen the body of young Davey and was heartbroken by a vital life force being cut so short.

When the accused stood before her, Mel was surprised at the gaunt woman. Insanity shone from her red tinted eyes. Her fangs were darkly stained with blood and uncleanliness. Mel was sickened by her, not only for her crimes, but for what she had allowed herself to become.

"Marta Lipscomb, you were summoned to this court on charges of magical misuse. Included in these charges are using magic to murder, kidnap, usage of black or dark magic and coercion. The lesser but no less serious breaches of conduct are attempted murder, theft, and rape. The punishment for each of these charges is death to be carried out forthwith. What do you say to these charges?"

"Misuse of magic?" The look of shock might have been comical had it not been so pathetic. "Don't be ridiculous. I've never…there isn't anyone alive to…there has to be a mistake. You and I are going to be great friends, my lady. You'll soon wish you hadn't said those things to a friend. Who dares say such things? I demand to know who my accuser is."

"Bring in the witnesses." Mel nodded to the guard next to her.

And from across the room a large double door was opened by two royal court guards. There was silence for a few long seconds as no one moved, and then heavy footsteps could be heard approaching the door.

With guards on each side of the line of people, in walked the line of witnesses. The line split once as they came upon the rows of chairs just to the left of the long table, dividing the guards from their company. All of the witnesses sat at the same time, save one. One person remained standing, staring at the woman at the podium. Mel watched Sam's face as she stared.

"Sam, honey you need to sit down. Sam," Aaron, who sat next to her, demanded in a whisper.

Mel could see that Sam was in shock, but she couldn't tell what she was in shock about. Mel could feel her emotions, but all she could get was numbness, which Mel couldn't understand. No one else would know her feelings with the exception of the Guard and her grandmother. It was because as soon as one entered the Courts, all magical ability was blocked as a safety precaution.

Aaron reached up and yanked her down to the seat next to his, pulling her onto Thomas Reilly, the vampire doctor, who was treating Jason and had performed the autopsy on Davey. Thankfully, Thomas didn't protest about having a woman in his lap, but shifted over to the seat that Sam should have taken. Aaron snapped his fingers in front of her face, and finally, when that didn't work, he shook her hard rattling her head about. Mel watched carefully as Sam turned to Aaron.

~~~

Sam looked up at Aaron, her eyes filled with unshed tears, her face as pale as death. He was suddenly very afraid that something had happened to Tucker, as he knew that mates could feel when the other was gravely injured or killed. "Sam?"

Her voice was barely a whisper, and with torment in her heart, she said, "It's her. That woman, it's her. She killed us. She's the last one."

Aaron looked at the vampire in the seat across from the table. He then looked at Mel. Neither of them knew what Sam meant, but a commotion at the other end of the room brought his thoughts to a stop.

They wheeled Tucker in on a very large gurney, the size no doubt to accommodate him, wheeled because he was so weak. When he was close enough to see that Aaron still had his hands on Sam, Tucker growled, the sound low and coming from deep within him. Aaron dropped his hand immediately. He looked over at the vampire and bowed. Aaron was shocked at the way his new friend looked.

"I'm sorry, but she is distressed about something or someone, I'm not sure. She said that 'she killed us.' I was just trying to figure out what she meant and to offer comfort in your absence." He might as well have been talking to the gurney itself for all the good it was doing him. The moment the two of them saw each other, everyone ceased to exist.

Tucker opened his arms for Sam and she ran to him, throwing him back against the bed. He started kissing her; every exposed bit of skin was tasted and licked. He nuzzled deep in her neck, where her shoulder met, and breathed deep, opening his mouth to take more of her in. He was about to sink his canines into her when Aaron pulled them apart. He yanked Sam from Tucker so abruptly that he nearly fell from the bed. As Tucker was reaching to bring her back, Aaron nodded toward the woman, Marta, who was screaming now.

"Get that fucking bitch away from my mate. I'll kill you, you hear me, and I'll kill you both for what you've done. Let me go. I said to let me go now." Marta was trying to get to the young couple, but the guard held her in place. The pathetic woman dressed up in a ridiculous costume was gone. In her place was a crazed maniac.

"Guards! Guards! Restrain her, this instant," Mel commanded sharply. When she was subdued and order once again maintained, the queen started again.

"If there is one more outburst, I will deem this court unnecessary and make the proclamation myself. And Marta, you so don't want to piss me off any more than I already am. First witness, Thomas Reilly. You! Sit and shut up. Begin." Aaron felt Mel's power move through the room and had to cover a quick chuckle when poor Thomas looked ready to wet himself.

"Yes, of course. Forgive me, 'begin' what exactly? I've never been...this is my first time in this court, your ladyship. And while I know it's a great honor to be called, I'm as nervous as a whore in a room full of...well, I'm nervous," Thomas said with a slight laugh. Aaron actually felt sorry for him.

~~~

"You may do well to have the young couple pulled away so that she may feed him. I can feel his hunger from here," Elizabeth whispered through Mel's mind.

"No, I can't." Mel wanted to, wanted to help the young vampire very badly. "I feel there is a reason he must remain weak and hungry. Something one of the Fates said before I came in here. 'Hunger shouldn't be fed, weakness will show great strength.' I don't know what is means. Whoever does with those three? But as soon as I felt his, I knew he was the one they were talking about. I just don't understand how great power will arrive with him being so very weak."

"Hummm, who knows, but you are probably right. Let's see what the bitch in front of us does next." Mel could practically see her grandmother rubbing her hands together in excitement.

"Please tell all who will listen what you found when you were called to the Brotherhood of Gray's pack house two days ago," Mel continued to the doctor.

"I arrived at the house because I had gotten a call from Aaron MacManus, Master Vampire of this Realm to come and aid the medical team to try and save the life of one Jason Alexander March, age fifteen." Mel nodded when Thomas hesitated. "It was determined that without the ability to shift into his true form, a werewolf, he would die. His body had one hundred and fifty-three stab wounds covering nearly his entire frame, all approximately one to three inches deep. He had lost a great deal of his blood, as he had been turned upside down and tied to a tree like a gutted pig. He had been hanging there, oh, about two hours, I'd guess. Had he been there much longer, we'd be making two funeral arrangements instead of just the one. After he was stabilized, and beginning to heal, I was asked to determine the cause of death for another young were. David Macklin March, sixteen and cousin to the other boy, was deceased. His throat had been ripped from him and he bled to death. Prior to his death, he had been eviscerated and his face had been ripped open by a deep set of claws. His death had been slow and horrific. His suffering was great, I would imagine."

The Courts of Magic was different from the human courts. One could get emotionally involved in here, and no one objected, well, not too much. Thomas was enjoying himself, Mel could tell. Not the story itself, but by telling a room full of people just how much he had witnessed and how it made him feel. Aaron would hear about his day in court for centuries, she was sure.

"When you say eviscerated, what do you mean precisely?" Mel knew he was sure what had happened. She had seen the young boys herself. It was a sight she would never forget. But the rest of the Court, they had not. She wanted them to have a clear picture of what had happened to him, leaving no doubt what the youth had suffered.

"Disemboweled, as in his stomach and all of the other organs, liver, intestines, had spilled from an open wound, caused by the same set of deep claws. He was still alive when this took place. He would have had to have been in deep pain and the loss of blood would have made him weaker. He didn't die easily. Poor boy."

"He cried for his mommy, the little cock sucker," Marta said calmly. "That's probably what he was going to do to the little one, get him down and suck him off. You're all lucky I came along and put a stop to that. World does not need more of their kind breeding. Vampires are the one and true race and the rest of you are only food." Marta was actually proud that she had killed an innocent kid, Mel realized. Proud and wondering why the others couldn't understand what she had done was a good thing.

"Enough. You will not say another word until you are asked to. Do I make myself understood?" Mel was sickened by her and wanted her to shut the fuck up.

"If I had my magic, you'd be one sorry bitch, you understand that?" Marta said to her.

The Royal Guard moved forward as one, ready to kill the insolent vampire. But a raised hand from Mel stopped them. This was one of the main reasons the queen was to keep her magic when everyone else couldn't. She and her champion were the only things that stood between an all-out blood bath and order, or semi-order. But Mel knew the woman had to be silenced.

"You will not speak again until I give you leave." As soon as the words left Mel's mouth, Marta's mouth disappeared.

Mel was not a cruel leader, but she was inventive when it came to making people believe she was just what she was, a power like none other, someone to be reckoned with.

"Is there anything else, Dr. Reilly?" Elizabeth was nearly crying from holding back her laughter and Mel wanted to desperately to smack her to get her to stop snorting with it.

"No. No, I think that's all. I mean…Christ, that's scary. I mean…I believe I've said…I'm done, your majesty."

Mel felt sorry for Thomas. The poor man was "freaked out," as she'd heard Mac say once. Thomas kept stealing glances at Marta, no doubt worried she'd do the same thing to him if he misspoke.

"Next on the list is Tucker James. Tucker, would you be able to testify from there?" Mel asked him with a gentle smile. But before he could answer, Sam stood up.

"If it pleases the court, I would like to testify for him, my lady. He is my mate, contrary to some people's opinion." Sam glared at Marta before turning back to her. "And I would very much like to also be able to hear her comments when I'm done."

"If Tucker has no objections, then I don't see anything wrong with it." At Tucker's nod, Mel waved her hand at Sam. "You may proceed."

Sam made her way to the table, but stopped briefly to touch Tucker. Love swelled around those closest to the couple. Mel looked sharply at her grandmother, wondering if she had felt the magic too. From the look on her face, she would say that she had. Curious.

"Marta Lipscomb murdered my mother and me when I was a child. She was with five other people when she did." Sam looked at the council. They looked shocked and somewhat bewildered. "I mean, she murdered my mother and I was dead as well until, using the last of her magic, she healed me and saved my life."

"You're mother, what was her name and what was she?" Elizabeth asked.

"A very powerful Magi, mistress. Her name was Constance Hunter. She at one time was a member of these proceedings. She once served as counsel to the fairy queen." Sam bowed low. "She spoke very highly of you, mistress. She said you were a woman to trust and one not to piss off."

With a burst of laughter, Elizabeth answered Sam. "Yes, I remember your mother. I hadn't heard that she had died. I'm very sorry for your loss, young lady. The others that night, I'd like to have their names, please. We will be able to locate them and bring them to justice as well if Marta is found guilty of her crimes." Elizabeth picked up a pen and waited for Sam to tell her. Aaron leaned forward and waited.

"Of course, but justice has been served. All of them, save this one, are dead. They were Shirley Max, Simon Dale, Dan and Steven Pickett—brothers—and Robert Peterson."

CHAPTER TWENTY

The room erupted in voices. Murmurs of names and deeds of the dead could be heard, more of how the girl must surely be lying. One so young could not have killed such violent creatures.

Mel and her grandmother put their heads together for a moment then conferred with the other members of the Council of Nine. After a few more minutes, one of the nine turned to Sam.

"I am Skilika. I am a white witch of old. I would like more information on the death of Shirley Max. How did she die?" Mel nodded for her to continue when Sam looked up.

"When I found her, she was in a cabin just outside of Michigan where she was abusing a little boy. He was being used a...he was...she was cutting off different areas of his skin—my lady, are the details necessary?" Sam asked suddenly.

Sam didn't think anyone would want the details of that day. She didn't and she'd been there. "Yes, Sam Hunter, the details if you please. I know this will be hard to be heard, but I believe it will go a long way in having justice served. Continue."

"The woman was cutting off different areas of his skin and eating it. I believe she thought that it would make her younger. I was...I subdued her and took the little guy to the nearest hospital and left him in their care. It seemed that his parents had sold him to her for the ability to cast spells. After I...saw to his family, I then went back and peeled her skin from her body. And before you ask, yes, she was still alive."

"You killed her, alone? That is quite unheard of, you know. She was a strong witch of the dark arts. Yet you claim to have killed her alone. How do I believe you?" Skilika asked.

Sam closed her eyes, brought up the memory of the witch Shirley, and sent the image to her, complete with the screams. Skilika staggered back as if slapped. She sat down hard in the chair that was directly behind her or she would have fallen. She turned her stricken face to the queen.

"She gave me the image, the memory, my queen. She sent it to me. I thought only you were to use magic during these proceedings."

Sam felt the queen's touch, her search of magic. Sam knew she wouldn't find any because what she could do wasn't just magic but the ability to control her mind and those of others. She'd been able to do this before that night, only now it was stronger.

"What I use isn't magic, it's simple mind control. I have the ability to use my mind in ways that defy anything medical doctors have ever seen. When one of the men shot me in the head, they woke up a long dormant part of the brain and activated all sorts of freaky things." Sam bowed before the queen. "I would give it up if only I could."

"We will discuss this at a later time. I have searched her for any usage of power, and it is as she says, she has none. Are you satisfied, Skilika?"

"Yes, my lady, but I would like to know of the body of the witch, and of the parents." Skilika still sat down. Sam almost felt sorry for her.

"As would I," Elizabeth said softly.

"Her body will never be found. It has become a part of the earth by now. My mother taught me the earth needs to be repaid tenfold, whether or not you use it. The parents..." Sam smirked slightly. "They met with a terrible accident not long after Ryland was found. They too have paid the earth."

"Dan and Steven Pickett, what of them?" asked another of the nine. "They were vampires, not really old, but powerful none the less. I know that before they left my realm, they had started using the darker magic as well, sacrificing small and sometimes larger animals. And please, don't send me anything. I promise I will believe you." The man chuckled. "I'm Roman Stall, master in another realm. Aaron knows me. We've been friends longer than either of us care to count."

Sam looked at Aaron and waited. He smiled back at her and nodded. She wasn't sure she liked that smile, but turned back to the vampire before her.

"Steven died in his car in Chicago. I caught him draining a woman in an alley. I couldn't stop him from killing the woman, I'm so sorry about that. But he died as she did. I wrapped him in silver, then sliced his throat and watched him bleed out. Dan was lake fishing with Simon Dale, he was a werewolf. They were in the middle of Lake Erie when fifty sticks of dynamite went off beneath the chairs they were seated on. They had two women locked in a shed about two miles from them that they had been using as food. One had been drained completely. The other woman had been sexually assaulted and abused so much that she ate her own wrist open and killed herself. I don't know who they were. I could never find any missing reports that fit their description. If it would help, I could give you their images and the search could be widened."

"If they were human, unfortunately I would have no way of finding any more information than you did. I do, however, thank you for your help. I am indebted to you, as is my Kiss." With a nod of his head, he sat down.

Bradley stood up and faced Sam. She was afraid of this man's questions. She knew him, had dealings with his pack. If he wished it, she couldn't stay with Tucker in Aaron's Kiss.

"If I may, mistress, Peterson's death is of interest to me. As you are aware, he was found guilty of murdering a little girl, Becca, some years ago. I would very much like to hear only what became of him, how he died."

"I know of Becca, as you are aware. And to finally lay to rest the information concerning the man who killed her is very dear to my heart as well." Mel wiped at tears in her eyes. "Sam, please tell us what you know of her murderer."

Sam looked over at Tucker. At his nod, she turned back to the council. Any and all of the murders that she had committed would easily result in her own death. Before meeting Tucker, she wouldn't have cared at all, would have welcomed it really. But now she wondered what her answer would be if asked if she wanted to die.

"I couldn't find him when I searched here for him. I knew of...I'd heard of the young human's life he'd taken. He wasn't...men like him need to be extinguished from this earth." Sam took a deep breath before continuing. "He was...he had a harem of young children in a large house just outside of California. There were several dozen children and four 'house mothers' there who took care of them and when necessary, got rid of the bodies when his play got a little too rough. If you are interested, the house is still standing, but no longer in use. I saw to that. I...he was stronger than the others. I've never dealt with a wolf before, not like him. Simon was a smallish one, and too stupid to be afraid, but Peterson wasn't. I was able to get him to shift by fucking...err, messing with his mind. He believed it to be a full moon, you see. Once he was in wolf form, I tranked him with enough drugs to take down a large bear. I waited until he woke several hours later to kill him. I had staked him to the ground deep in a wild area of a forest preserve. He had shifted back to human when he fell over, so I covered his body from head to toe with enough silver to keep him immobile. Then I cut him, sliced him open in several smaller veins and nicked a larger vein in his leg. He was eaten alive by the animals that roamed the grounds. They were attracted by the smell of his blood. It took them several days to finish him off, but he was dead after the third day."

Bradley stared at Sam. She knew what she had done was cruel, heartless even, but she wouldn't change anything if she could. He'd been a monster, a monster that preyed on children. When Bradley started toward her, Sam didn't flinch or back away. She would take what he gave her and not give them the satisfaction of begging for mercy. But Bradley walked to her and hugged her to him. Hugged her until she returned the hug herself.

"Thank you." Was all he said to her before he walked back to the chair.

No one spoke; not one person moved for several long, tense minutes. Mel looked at the council and they back at her. Sam knew they were both repulsed and intrigued by her. This little slip of a girl with no magical powers at all had managed to kill five very powerful beings. And in ways that seemed oddly justified to each monster. But she had done what she had felt was necessary.

"My lady? I would hear what the vampire Marta Lipscomb has to say for her part in all this," the centaur asked.

Mel nodded. "You may speak, Marta. But you'll keep a civil tongue in your head."

And without any warning at all, Marta flew at Tucker.

The guards moved toward Marta, but before they could descend on them, she had Tucker's throat exposed and her mouth moving to his vein. She froze suddenly, her fangs extended a mere half an inch from biting him. She trembled with the strain of trying to bite, to finish him off, but she couldn't seem to do it.

"I will have him, he's mine. Do you hear me? He's mine." Marta was snarling at Sam as she continued to strain against the hold.

"Everyone hears you. Hell, people outside can probably hear you. But he's mine," Sam said calmly. "Now, either back the fuck away from him or I will destroy you."

Sam hadn't moved one inch. No one had since the guard had surrounded Tucker and her with their weapons at the ready. Sam looked straight at Marta, afraid to look at Tucker, afraid if she did then she would lose her hold on the woman who could very well kill what Sam now considered hers.

"You think to harm me? Me? I'm the greatest vampire ever to live. You all should be bowing before me not this...this imposter." Marta glanced toward Mel. "I have killed more humans than all of you combined, and I will rid the world of more. You are nothing but sheep, baaing your way through life, just waiting for someone like me to come along and end your miserable existence. I will take and take, and there is nothing you can do to stop me." Marta pushed harder to take his throat. Sam was having a hard time not just killing the bitch. But then she backed away. Suddenly, she extended her fingers into sharp talons and stretched them toward Sam.

"Yeah, yeah, you are the greatest. Blah, Blah, Blah. No one gives a shit." At least Sam hoped so. "You have one minute to back the fuck up, or die. I'm being nice to you because there are too many witnesses to take your skinny ass out right now. But all bets are off if you try and touch Tucker again. You hear me, bitch?"

Sam felt the touch, so light that she might have imagined it, and then she moved along her mind.

"Mistress?" The queen was just on the edges of her mind and Sam had to hold harder on Marta or lose her. "Now isn't really a good time for me, my lady. Do you think maybe we could do this a—"

"Sam, is that you against her? Are you holding her with your mind?" Mel asked her.

"Not really." Sam felt the tiny bit of magic touch her and wondered about it. "She just thinks I am. That's the thought that I've pushed at her, that she can't harm him, it's impossible to harm him. Her mind isn't weak, but I can win this."

"I offer you my assistance," the queen said. "Because you are not using magic so by my law, you are breaking none."

"I...I love Tucker, my lady, and would not have my actions reflect upon him. I thought that when this day came, when I could kill those who hurt us, who took my mom away from me, that I'd willingly sacrifice myself as well, but I can't. I can't leave Tucker."

"Well of course you do, love," Mel told her with a chuckle. "You are his true mate. Now I want you to do something for me. Do you think you could trust me, and do one thing for me?"

"I...trust? I don't have a lot of faith in people. To trust is very hard for me, no offense. But I will hope that you will do right by me. I'm sorry...very sorry, but that's the best I can do." Sam was getting weaker. Her mind was tired.

"Good enough. For now anyway. You and I will work on the rest. And I do appreciate your honesty. I will need you to do me a favor, later. For now, let's you and I fry this fucking bitch."

Sam smiled. For the first time in many, many days, she smiled. "Ah, now that's an easy one, my lady. How do you like your bitch? Extra crispy or original?"

~~~

Marta was running the sharp talons along Tucker's neck. She couldn't seem to make herself tear through the tender flesh. She just kept staring at it and straining to just cut. Her mind cleared for a moment. She felt so...so...happy. Happy? No, exuberant, intoxicated, content almost, yes, that's the way she felt. She had everything, her life was perfect. Now was the time, she thought. It cannot get any better than this, I can just go.

The blades on her fingers stopped caressing Tucker. She leaned back away from him and looked at him. If asked, Tucker would swear that she had the most beautiful look on her face. She was tranquil.

Her fingers, blades really, moved up along her hip and across her abdomen, cutting and tearing at her clothes, nicking her flesh in places as she walked several feet from Tucker. Moving up along her front across her chest, she sliced open her dress, exposing the corset beneath. The sharpness of her blades cut through the fabric and lacings to the skin and muscle underneath. She was bleeding now, from dozens of cuts and slices. She didn't seem to notice any of this, and her eyes closed, the smile serene, her head tilted back. And still she moved upward, closer to her neck and face. When she reached her throat, her body was all but exposed to those gathered in the room, but none saw the woman there, only the destruction of madness.

"I deserve this. I'm going to be rewarded for my good deeds toward mankind. They will thank me and erect a statue in my honor for showing them the way." She opened her eyes and looked straight into Sam's dark, dark purple ones, and sliced her own throat open, nearly severing her head from her shoulders.

As she fell to the ground, Sam released her hold on the woman. It was only then that she realized that Sam had killed her. Sam stepped toward the fallen woman, stepping in her blood as if it meant so little to her, and said to her in a loud voice so that there would no misunderstanding.

"He's mine, you fucking bitch." And then, Marta incinerated.

CHAPTER TWENTY-ONE

Sam threw herself at Tucker, kissing and touching any exposed skin she could reach. The tears running down her face were mixing with his. His joy at having her, of her being there, was overwhelming to her.

"Sam, baby, I love you. I love you so very much. Be mine, let me be yours. Please, baby, say yes."

"Yes, yes, yes, yes, yes. I love you too."

Aaron cleared his throat again, and then again before the couple looked up at him with a sort of dazed, hungry look about them.

"You know, fang face, I'm getting sick of you doing that. You should really see a doctor or take a couple of cough drops to clear that up," Sam said with a glare. It was the second time since they'd come into this room he had tried to break them apart.

"Be that as it may, the mistress would like to see you; these proceedings are not quite finished."

The couple pulled apart, but not away from each other. Mel had a sly grin on her face that said, "I know you are pissed, but tough, I'm in charge."

"Sam Hunter, you are hereby charged in the murder and destruction of six beings. You will now be judged by the masters of those beings. Stand before us."

Sam knew that there was a very good possibility that she would be brought to justice someday for her crimes. She moved to stand before the council, but was momentarily shocked by those who stood behind her; her Tucker was there as well. She looked to the queen for guidance and she winked at her. Actually winked! Then the judging began.

"I Skilika, Watcher of White Magic, in the name of the Queen, Mistress of the Light, Keeper of Magic, do hereby drop all charges against Sam Hunter in the death of Shirley Max, witch of my realm. I would further like to thank Sam Hunter for her help and good, sound judgment in destroying someone so evil for all kind."

Sam staggered slightly, and if not for Tucker standing just behind her, may have fallen on her butt. He caressed his thumb across her skin, sending her his love through a tight hold around her waist.

"I, Roman Stall, Master Vampire of the Holland Realm, and in the name of the Queen, Mistress of the Light...is this really necessary, mistress? We all know that she isn't guilty, and even without magic, I can feel the sexual tension between these two like a thick ass fog. Let them go. I mean, haven't they both suffered about enough?" There was a very long pause, and then as if he just realized what he'd done, Roman looked up at the queen and with a little smile meant to soften his words, said, "That is, if it pleases the queen?"

"Very nice of you to remember your place, Roman Stall, but I see and feel your point. Does anyone object to waiving the sentencing of Sam Hunter? No? Then I hereby order you two to the Royal Suite to rest, eat, feed and recuperate. Court dismissed. Thanks, gang."

~~~

Tucker lay on the bed, and it was a very large bed doubled the width and length of two king-sized mattresses. But it fit the room. It was massive, as were the furnishings. The room looked like an entire floor of a house it was so big, and was furnished accordingly.

There were antiques and modern things that included, aside from the bed and dresser, a couch and two chairs that sat before a fireplace one could roast an ox in. There was a writing desk with a computer on it and the biggest closet he'd ever seen.

He was waiting for Sam; she had gone into the bathroom as soon as they had arrived and before the guard who had carried him in had left. He was beginning to worry and was just starting to rise and check on her when he heard the door open.

"Sam, honey, are you...fuck! Baby." Every drop of his blood rushed out of his body to settle in his cock in the time it took him to take a breath.

"Do you like it?" She turned around for him and the view was even more delicious from that angle. "I've never owned anything like this before, but Pete said that I had a mate now and should stop buying my undergarments from Wal-Mart. I told her I didn't, but she said it was an inside joke that she'd tell me about someday. Anyway, she said that I should make sure you and I strike a bargain."

"Yes. I agree to your terms, now come here, Sam. Now, come here and let me get a closer look."

She giggled as she moved to him, walking slowly across the room. She looked so good, and he could feel her hunger for him. He wanted her, all of her. When she was a foot from him and stopped, he growled low and deep in his chest.

"You know neither the terms nor the bargain, Tucker. How do you know that you agree?"

"If you come to me wearing anything remotely like this and ask me for something, it's yours. I don't care what I'll have to do to get it for you. Anything." He would, too, just for another look at her like this.

She looked tasty, like any man's deepest fantasy. The teddy was dark blue, almost the purple of her eyes. The bodice was tight across her ample breasts, pushing them up and spilling them over the top, barely covering her nipples. The laces down the front were tied tight, accentuating her tiny waist and flared hips, the top of it ending just below her ribs, showing off her hip bones. The panties were a tiny scrap of lace the same color as the top, which was a triangle just over her pussy and tied together with small strings at her hips. He reached out, put his hands on her hips, and tugged her forward.

"This is going to look so lovely in a scrap on the floor, Sam. I cannot wait to rip it from your body and eat you." His voice was deep with sexual need and hunger. Her body responded to both, flooding her already wet panties. The scent of her spiked his hunger more.

"Oh God, Tucker, please." She moved closer at his urging, and straddled his hips when he pulled her over him and onto the bed. "Please, I can't think...I...there's something I need to...oh God, yes, do that again."

He touched her pussy with his finger, pushing deep against the folds of her femininity, and felt her heat through the panties. She began to ride his hand, soaking it with her juices. He pulled her over to his hips and held her there as he let go of her hip to unsnap his pants. His need to be inside of her nearly consuming him, he could think of only that. When he got them open, he cock sprang free into his fist.

"Come here, Sam. I'm hungry for you. I want to sip from you and drink of your essences."

She scooted closer, her hands joining his on his cock, wrapping her fist around him as he surged into her. Reaching down to the strings of her panties, he yanked, rending the material into pieces. She rose on her knees the same moment he shifted her up and with her help guiding him, he sank her down on his cock.

Heat. Hot molten heat wrapped around him. He cried out at the sensation. Sitting up slightly, he pulled her down and flipped them over onto the mattress. He kissed her then, devoured her mouth, her taste, and more heat. He moved inside of her, stroking her deep and hard at the same time he moved along her jaw toward her throat. He wasn't going to last, he realized, and tried to slow down, to buy them more time. Just when he thought he was going to be able to last a minute or two longer, she nuzzled his neck and bit, hard. His control snapped, he licked her vein, and sank his teeth into her just as he came. With every draw from her body by his mouth, he slammed into her, his seed spewing and filling her. When he felt her tighten around him again, her climax clutching him and pulling him deeper into her body, he came again, roaring out his release and slamming into her.

CHAPTER TWENTY-TWO

It was two full days before the couple came up for air, enjoying each other and their love. Someone had been leaving food outside the door for them, platters of fruit and cheeses. Twice there was a large steak, rare with all the trimmings. They savored the food as much as they did each other. He fed from her, his body strengthened and sated.

When they met Mel in the late evening on the second day, she had gifts for them. Actually, they were mostly for Sam, but two for Tucker to share.

"This is for you, Sam. It was your mother's essence and her power base. It came back to me after you killed Marta. As a mage's daughter, you have some, although wholly untouched magic from her, but this will give you so much more. As I had the room devoid of magic, it came to me when Marta died. I wish for you to have it. It's white and pure, as was your mother."

"I...what do I want with it? Magic killed her, and hasn't done anyone I've seen any good. I don't want it." Sam backed away from the large, glowing orb that rested in Mel's hand.

Mel knew that Sam would feel this way and wasn't surprised when she wouldn't take it. But sometimes things had a way of doing what they wanted. "Be that as it may, it is yours." Suddenly, the orb jumped from her hand and straight into Sam, causing her to stiffen and shudder. But as quickly as it had entered her, the rush of it was over. Sam looked at Mel with a curious face.

"I guess it didn't work." Sam looked relieved.

Mel simply smiled. "Hmmmm, we'll see. But the magic knew to go to you, Sam. I didn't have anything to do with that part. When you backed away from it, the magic went to its home, to you."

Sam only shrugged her shoulder and looked at Tucker and what he was holding. Mel thought, Time will tell for this one.

"That is from Shawn. I was telling him about your story while the two of you...rested." Mel pointed to the package in Tucker's hand. "You didn't actually meet him. He's a centaur from another realm. This is his way of saying thanks. It's a travel charm. You just rub it gently and think about where it is you want to go, and you are there. It works for other realms besides Earth too. He would like you to visit him sometime."

Shawn had fallen for the girl, her bravery and single-minded determination impressing him more than he had been in centuries by any other being. He'd told Mel when she'd finished telling him all that they'd endured. And he had been impressed by Tucker, as well. With Tucker being a vampire, Shawn had expected him to leap to take Sam out of the fray, but instead, he let her save him. A rarity for a male to do, more so for a vampire.

It was a beautiful stone of the most brilliant yellow Mel had ever seen. The chain was gold with interlocking circles in a long coil. It looked to be heavy, but was actually quite light, and as soon as Sam put the chain around her neck, it glowed against her skin. Mel could actually see the magic it gave off.

"I believe these two are for you both. They are pledge guarantees." Mel handed them both scrolls. "It seems that if you do not wish to stay with Aaron as you're master, or he does not wish to accept you as his, then Roman and Peter, both masters of their own realms as well, have offered you a home and a job. You need only to come before them and pledge your alliances to one of them."

"Do you think that...I mean, did the master say that?"

Mel reached out and gentled the large vampire. It never occurred to her that Tucker would think that Aaron didn't want him. She wished that she had thought to ask Aaron about his intentions toward the man. "I wouldn't worry about that happening if I was you, Tucker. He sent messages six times yesterday asking about you two, and then today he demanded that I break down the door to make sure you hadn't killed each other. I told him that if the screams were any indication, then you were both...hummm...enjoying yourselves quite nicely."

Mel could feel their embarrassment and pride from Tucker. The man practically glowed with good health and wellbeing. For that matter, so did Sam. They had gotten loud and they had enjoyed each other, several times a day for two glorious days and nights, Mel knew. Hell, the entire court did as well.

Mel dismissed them soon after. She could see that they needed each other and would for a very long time to come. She hoped that they would visit her often, having felt a bond with them she hadn't felt in centuries.

~~~

Sam and Tucker lay on the bed, both sated for the moment. During their time together, they had talked a great deal. She had told him everything about herself, her abilities and the abused people she helped. He also knew that she baked and decorated because it was a way for her to decompress and relax. He told her about Marta and what she had done to him, how she had used and abused him and others. Some of the things that they had each done and had done to them were shared and they both felt better for sharing them for the first time.

Tucker also told Sam what she was now, an immortal as was he. He also explained that she would need to keep up her strength, as he would only feed from her for all eternity.

"Eating rare meats and drinking plenty of fluids will keep the two of us healthy." Tucker was stroking her skin as she lay naked before him.

"Will I feed from you? Grow fangs, I mean?"

His eyes turned at the thought of her drinking from him, her teeth sinking into his flesh. His cock hardened. His fangs elongated more. "Would you like that, Sam, to feed from me? Would you like to bite me? Feel me fill you?" His voice, along with his eyes, had turned; it was deeper with his need. He found that he wanted that, her to bite him soon, now as a matter of fact.

For an answer, she leaned into his body and buried her face into his throat, drawing deep the scent of him. She licked his pounding pulse and then pulled it into her mouth and bit him gently, then nipped harder.

"Christ, Sam. That's it, baby, bite me. Hard, bite me hard, baby."

He surged toward her, moving over her and pushing her onto her back as she nuzzled his neck. When she opened her mouth wider and then bit him, opening the vein with a tiny wound, he was already pushing his cock deep into her wetness. He came with a roar, bringing her with him, his blood filling her mouth, his cock filling her body. When he was able to move again, he showed her how to seal the small wound and lay back with her spread across his body. Both slept only to wake and start again.

~~~

They were seated in the kitchen when Tucker and Sam arrived later that evening at the MacManus mansion. Bradley had even come over to welcome them home.

"I do hope that you will accept my gratitude and heartfelt thanks for what you did for us. Disposing of such garbage was something that I will never be able to repay you for. And as such, I offer you my pledge as an alpha wolf; you now and forever will be an honorary pack member. Pack takes care of pack. Thank you again, Sam. Tucker." With a nod to Sara and Aaron, Bradley left them. Tucker decided to get this over with

"Sam and I have bonded truly, sire." Tucker started. "I wish to speak to you. We have offers of becoming a part of two other realms. They have told us that we could come there and live, with a job. I feel I must provide for my mate. I want to thank you for your support. We couldn't have…we would have died without you. If there is nothing else, we will be going."

The couple had talked about this as well as they made their way to the estate. Tucker wanted to start over, to start fresh, and Sam agreed with him. She wanted to go where he did, and her baking could be done from anywhere.

"No. I think not," Aaron said. He didn't move, not even when Sam turned on him.

"Hey, fang face, you don't tell us what to do. He doesn't…we don't belong to your little…whatever, and I'm not so sure I'd want to. You are the pushiest person I've ever met. And you! You are the bossiest woman I've ever known." Her last statement was directed right at Sara.

Aaron merely smiled at her. Then he turned his attention to his mate. When Sara gave him a slight nod, Aaron stood and advanced toward Sam, backing her against the furthest wall. Sara held Tucker still with magic so he couldn't come to her aid. When Aaron had Sam pressed against the wall, he grabbed her around the throat and lifted her from the floor. Tucker roared with anger.

"Use it, Sam. Use your power," Aaron demanded of her. "Throw me away and save Tucker." Tucker watched helplessly as Aaron squeezed the life out of Sam.

"No matter how long it takes, no matter how hard you fight, I'll kill you for this," Tucker growled at Aaron.

Tucker was being slammed against the opposite wall over and over as his mate died. Aaron pulled her away from the wall slightly and slammed her hard twice.

Suddenly, he was across the room in a heap; his nose bloodied his arm at an odd angle.

"Oh, my God, what have I done?" Sam ran to him and helped Tucker up, as Sara had dropped him as soon as Aaron flew across the room. Tucker knew Sam was in trouble the way Sara glared at her. Standing in front of Tucker to protect him, Sam raised her chin.

"You touch him and I'll kill you, you piece of —"

"You inherited the power base that was Marta's, Sam. Your mother was Magi, and by killing her, Marta took her powers. You, in turn, took her powers and they became yours. Mel told us that the base went to you. Everyone that she ever killed, their power base now is a part of you." Aaron's arm was already healing; his nose was wiped clean as he spoke to Sam.

"This was a test? Are you fucking nuts? I could have hurt you. Then what? Your mate would have tried to kill us. Well, I don't want it. Take it back. I...what am I supposed to do with it? Take it, you can have it."

Sara snorted. "Aaron, like me, is a true immortal. And yes, it was a test. More than you could know. Aaron and I have a deal for you. We'd like—"

"Fuck you and your deal. What the hell? You expect us to what...drop down and kiss your feet? I don't think so, toots. I thought I hated you before all this shit, now I—"

"Enough, Sam." Tucker could see now what they had been doing. They wanted to see Sam realize her powers, her gift.

"I...I don't want...I don't know how to make this work. Please, I just want to be with Tucker. That's all I want and to run my shop, bake cakes, and pretty things." Her head was suddenly spinning around, the room tilted oddly. "I'll not bother you again, not that I did in the first place."

"I'll show you how to use it, Sam. It would be my pleasure to show you. I know we haven't really gotten off to a good start, and I think that might be my fault—" Sara started only to be cut off by Sam.

"Think it might be your fault! You stuck your fucking finger in my bullet hole to prove a point. Yeah, I'd say we got off to a bad start. And it never got any better with your nosey, bossy ways."

Sara stiffened. "I was not being bossy. I was trying to help you. If I hadn't made you seek medical attention, you'd of never have met Tucker. And that—"

"Ladies, ladies. I would like to point out that you both are destroying the room as we speak." Aaron stood beside Tucker dodging items as they flew about the kitchen. Duncan, for once, was not in the vicinity.

Sam's hair was standing on end and objects were flying around the room. Just as Aaron pointed it out and she realized it, everything dropped to the floor.

"Oh, God, I'm so sorry. I'll pay for everything, I swear. I'm...I'm so...shit, I'm dizzy." And Sam hit the floor.

When she woke later, Tucker was leaning over her smiling. They were in the bedroom again, the one he knew she disliked.

"You know, I really, really hate this room. But if you promise not to leave me in here alone, I think I could stand it a little longer."

He kissed her before he spoke. "I've accepted Aaron's offer. And Sara is beside herself with worry about you. How do you feel?" Tucker couldn't stop from grinning at her.

"Let's see, stupid, overwhelmed, tired, hungry, pissy...let's just say I'm running the whole emotional spectrum right now. Why did you accept his offer? Not that I care, because it's you who has to deal with him, but why?"

He touched her again, ran his hand down her arm, and made her shiver. He knew he'd just added yet another emotion.

"Tucker, if you keep that up, we won't leave this bedroom before sunrise." He grinned at her.

"I love you, Sam. Did you know that Sara has a friend named Shade? You've met her, I believe. She came here when you fainted."

"I didn't faint. Why was she called in? She's their healer or something, right?"

"Or something." He touched her again. "Have I told you in the last two minutes that I love you. I do, very much. You're pregnant, love. That's why you...hummm...when you tripped over that air molecule while standing perfectly still and hit your head on something on the way to the floor —"

"Okay, I fainted. I'm pregnant? That's not possible. Is it? Well, I mean, we do go at it a lot. A baby? Tucker, I can't even care for...We're...a baby? I...is it okay with you? I...a baby? Wow."

He answered her with a kiss. A kiss that said he loved her and that it was more than okay with him that she was having his child, their child.

"I love you with all of my being; I will love you for all of my lives. I love you, Sam Hunter James."

ABOUT THE AUTHOR

I woke up one morning and decided to give play time to the people in my head who were keeping me awake. Little did I know that they would be so relentless and want their time right now! I wrote for the pure joy of it and to entertain my family and friends. But mostly it was to get more than an hour of sleep without a story playing out. Of course, the more I write, the more they want. So...well, as a result of sleepless days (I work through the night as a gun toting grandma - nope not a vigilantly but an armed security guard) I have lots of stories written.

Hello! My name is Kathi Barton and I'm an author. I have been married to my very best friend Sonny for at times seems several lifetimes – in a good way, honey. And together we have three wonderful children and then the ones we brought into the world - Paul and Dale Barton, Jason and Wendy Barton and Danielle and Ben Conklin. They have given us seven of the greatest treasures on Earth. They don't live at home seven days a week! No, seriously, seven grandchildren – Gavin, Spring, Ben, Trinity, Sarah, Kelly and Kian.